# How to Pursue a DNA Clue

## A MAGS AND BIDDY GENEALOGY MYSTERY BOOK SIX

### ELIZA WATSON

HOW TO PURSUE A DNA CLUE

Copyright © 2022 by Elizabeth Watson

All rights reserved by author.

Cover design by Lyndsey Lewellen at LLewellen Designs.

This is a work of fiction. Names, characters, places, brands, media, and incidents are either the product of the author's imagination or are used fictitiously. Any resemblance to actual events, locales, or persons, living or dead, is entirely coincidental.

ISBN-10: 1-950786-13-7 (ebook)

ISBN-13: 978-1-950786-13-8 (ebook)

ISBN-13: 978-1-950786-14-5 (paperback)

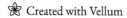 Created with Vellum

# Books by Eliza Watson

## NONFICTION
*Genealogy Tips & Quips*

## FICTION

### A Mags and Biddy Genealogy Mystery Series
*How to Fake an Irish Wake* (Book 1)

*How to Snare a Dodgy Heir* (Book 2)

*How to Handle an Ancestry Scandal* (Book 3)

*How to Spot a Murder Plot* (Book 4)

*How to Trace a Cold Case* (Book 5)

*How to Pursue a DNA Clue* (Book 6)

### The Travel Mishaps of Caity Shaw Series
*Flying by the Seat of My Knickers* (Book 1)

*Up the Seine Without a Paddle* (Book 2)

*My Christmas Goose Is Almost Cooked* (Book 3)

*My Wanderlust Bites the Dust* (Book 4)

*Live to Fly Another Day* (Book 5)

*When in Doubt Don't Chicken Out* (Book 6)

For additional books by Eliza Watson, visit
www.elizawatson.com.

Dear Reader,

In 2013 my husband, Mark, and I spent our first Christmas at our new home in Ireland. Since that time, friends and family have introduced us to their holiday traditions. I've enjoyed tasting my first Christmas pudding, pulling my first cracker and wearing its tissue-paper crown, and attending my first St. Stephen's Day celebration rather than fighting the crowds for after-Christmas bargains.

Mark and I have created a few Irish traditions of our own. We attend Christmas Mass at my ancestors' church. I dress up wine bottles in festive holiday outfits, including the pink bunny suit from *A Christmas Story*. My friend Mags displays the growing collection each Christmas in her dining room. Mark introduced our best friends, the Carters, to game-day chili on New Year's Eve. It was a huge hit and has become our annual dinner. We meet up with my Coffey relations Bernard and Nuala in Dublin for lunch and shopping. And buying gifts for my cousin Charlotte's two boys is always great craic.

In *How to Pursue a DNA Clue*, Mags Murray carries on holiday traditions passed down from her maternal grand-mother, as well as embracing new ones. You may find that a few of my own traditions make an appearance in the book.

At the end of the story, I've included a research article from my nonfiction book, *Genealogy Tips & Quips*: "Tracing Your Family Backward and Then Forward to Find Living Relatives."

I hope my tips inspire you to begin tracing your family tree or help you break down a brick wall!

Cheers!

Eliza Watson

*To my sister Kathy.*
*You have endured more losses and heartache*
*than any person ever should in a lifetime.*
*I hope you and Conner (1997–2022) both find peace.*

*Death leaves a heartache no one can heal;*
*love leaves a memory no one can steal.* —*Irish Proverb*

# One

No way were my best friend Biddy McCarthy and I having our mugshots taken while dressed as elves. The picture would go viral faster than the one of us supposedly digging up a skeleton at Halloween. Hopefully, nobody had recorded *this*...incident.

Gretta Lynch sat slumped in the chair next to us, looking like a seventy-five-year-old pregnant Mrs. Claus. The trim woman's attempt at plumping up her stomach with a pillow under her red velvet dress made her appear seven months pregnant. Thanks to her costume, a jar of whole nutmeg, and a gingerbread house, we were in the grocery store's security office. I debated calling in the favor Garda Higgins owed Biddy and me. Yet with our luck, we'd be in desperate need of a much bigger favor in the future.

Besides, Biddy and I were innocent, except that the nutmeg was for the Christmas pudding my friend Rosie was making for the holiday feast with both my dads. However, I hadn't told Gretta to snatch the last jar just as a mother with two toddlers was reaching for it. The kids had wailed at the top of their lungs, as if the combative Mrs. Claus had destroyed their belief in Christmas. The mother and Gretta ended up in a tug-of-war over the jar. Off balance, Gretta had grabbed a table displaying a three-foot-high gingerbread replica of Malahide Castle, and it had crashed to the floor with her. While Nurse Biddy had checked Gretta for broken bones, angry shoppers raced to the customer service desk and demanded a refund on their tickets for the gingerbread castle auction benefiting a toy drive.

Biddy eyed the store manager sitting behind the desk. A fortyish disheveled-looking woman whose holiday spirit was quickly fading as Biddy attempted to defend our actions. "Why isn't *freshly* grated nutmeg in the nuts section or produce section with fresh herbs? Searched a half hour before finding whole nutmeg in a display at the end of an aisle."

Who knew whole nutmeg came in a jar and you were responsible for grating it?

"Nutmeg isn't a *nut*," the manager snapped. "It's a *seed*."

Biddy tossed her arms up in frustration, swiping the deer-antlers headband from her blond hair, which was pulled back in a ponytail. "Then why not call it *seed*meg? If baking wasn't so bloody difficult, maybe I'd do it more often."

"You're not here to provide input on renaming the spice or where we should be displaying it." The woman's annoyed gaze narrowed on the colorful gumdrops clinging to Gretta's velvet dress and the sticky green icing on the white fur-trimmed cuffs.

"And don't even get me started on the fact that you're out of unfrosted shortbread cutout cookies and mixes," Biddy said.

"Buy frosted ones."

"Can't be frosting cookies that are already frosted, now can we?" Biddy snapped.

I had fond memories of helping Grandma Fitzsimmons frost her freshly baked shortbread cookies. After a few not-so-fond memories of myself unsuccessfully rolling out the dough, I'd decided unfrosted cookies were the stress-free way to go. Like eggnog, maybe unfrosted cutout cookies weren't as popular in Ireland as in the States.

The manager gave Biddy an exasperated eye roll. "It's nearly the holiday. Can't be expecting to find what you need at this late date."

Biddy jutted out her chin in defense. "Christmas isn't for ten days."

I placed a cautioning hand on Biddy's arm, visions of our mugshots, rather than sugarplums, dancing in my head. "Sorry. It's been a stressful day," I told the manager, massaging my throbbing foot that a young boy had run over with a truck, ripping the bells from my green pointy-toed elf bootie. I explained that we'd just come from handing out the presents Gretta had graciously donated to the hospital's pediatric ward where Biddy worked.

The manager appeared unimpressed with our good deed.

"We'd be happy to donate the extra gifts to the toy drive." I didn't mention there were only three.

A twinkle of interest shone in the woman's eyes. "That might be a start."

Gretta burst into tears. "I'll never"—she choked back a sob—"eat bloody nutmeg again. All my Christmas karma from donating gifts to charities is gone just like that, thanks to a jar of that wretched spice."

I slipped a comforting arm around the woman's narrow shoulders.

Thirty-one years ago, Gretta had insisted her eighteen-year-old unmarried daughter, Maeve, place her baby up for adoption. Unable to live with the regret, last month Gretta took a DNA test hoping to locate her grandson. Two days ago she'd received notification that her DNA had been analyzed. She was a complete basket case awaiting her list of matches.

So was I. It'd been two years since a DNA test had revealed my dad wasn't my biological father. My mom couldn't provide answers for my many questions, having died four years ago. I'd recently attended a Clan Murray family reunion in Scotland and discovered that my dad's second cousin, Ian Murray, was my bio father. Once the initial shock and awkwardness had worn off, the men got on great. They'd be visiting me for the holidays, the first anniversary of my maternal grandma's death. I had enough stress without the drama of Gretta discovering she'd been unknowingly switched at birth or that her mother was her dad's second cousin.

"Maybe you could be paying to have the gingerbread castle replaced," Biddy told Gretta. "Except the store is likely out of gumdrops, candy canes, and bloody flour."

Inspiration flickered in Gretta's gray eyes.

The manager scoffed. "We'd certainly have the necessary ingredients, except the sweets for decorating might be difficult to find at any store right now. Besides, it was to be auctioned off in two days. It'd never even be done by Christmas. A master baker and his assistants worked a week to create the castle."

"Could be having it as a New Year's giveaway," Biddy said.

Gretta nodded enthusiastically.

"The baker kindly donated his time, and the store contributed the ingredients for the original one. You'd have to fund the project."

Gretta's smile faded as she continued nodding. "No worries about the cost. 'Tis grand."

I turned to Gretta. "I'll help pay for it."

"Not only do I be needing to get karma back on my side but also the locals. I can't be known as *The Grinch Who Stole Christmas*."

Oddly, Gretta the Grinch had been one of my nicknames for the woman before she'd turned over a new leaf nearly a year ago—after unintentionally causing Finn O'Brien's car accident. And she was lucky I hadn't pressed charges when she'd knocked me unconscious with her purse and left me lying in a bush to prevent me from discovering the truth. She'd gotten off easy with a thousand community service hours.

The manager pushed herself up from the chair and heaved an exasperated sigh. "I suppose I could rethink involving the garda in the spirit of Christmas if you replace the castle and donate those presents you mentioned."

She agreed we could drop off the gifts tomorrow once people had calmed down and our lives weren't at risk. She offered to phone the baker to verify his availability and to provide a list of ingredients we could start tracking down.

We headed through the busy store trying to ignore customers' glares and attempts at snapping our pictures. The last thing we needed was another viral Twitter post. I'd be the

Toy Terminator instead of the Tombstone Terminator or Skeleton Scavenger—the nicknames I'd received after finding a dead man on my grandparents' grave and uncovering a skeleton at Halloween when pushing Biddy's car from the mud.

We escaped out to the parking lot and hopped into the safety of Biddy's car.

"I guess I'm going to have to give my grandma's short-bread cookies another shot," I said. Luckily, I had her rolling pin, cookie cutters, and recipe.

"I'd planned on giving Collin one of those extra pressies." Biddy gestured over her shoulder at the wrapped gifts in the backseat. "When he opened it to find a Barbie Doll or Elmo, I could have acted shocked, pretending I accidentally switched his present with one for the children's ward. Having to replace it would have bought me more time to figure out his bloody gift." Collin was Biddy's boyfriend.

Amazingly, I'd found the perfect gifts for Dad and Ian. Since they'd be opening their presents together, I'd decided to get them identical ones. That solved my worry over any awkwardness of getting one of them a better present than the other. They could use the Scottish blue monogrammed golf balls on their spring golf trip with Ian's brother, Tavish.

Wait a sec. That would be a bit awkward if Dad and Ian had personalized golf balls and Tavish didn't. I'd have to order my uncle a set.

"Can we make a run past the sweet shop?" Biddy asked. "Need to at least buy Collin some of that lovely honeycomb candy before there's a run on that also. He's taking me to a fancy hotel in Dublin for New Year's. I have to buy him more than sweets."

Gretta let out an excited squeal in the backseat, startling Biddy and me. Her gaze darted up from her cell phone, a glint of anticipation in her gray eyes.

The tiny hairs stood up on the back of my neck.

Her DNA matches had posted.

"Just a quick stop for sweets," Gretta said. "Need to be getting back to Mags's house."

My stomach tossed. I wished I was on my way to jail rather than home to analyze Gretta's DNA results.

## Two

No DOORBELL TO RING, Gretta pounded a fist against the blue wooden door on Rosie's white bungalow, nearly shaking the holly wreath from its nail.

Biddy flinched, rolling her eyes. "You're going to be crushing the bones in your hand."

She was still upset about Gretta snatching the box of honeycomb candy from her hand and marching it to the checkout counter because Biddy was *dawdling*.

The door flew open. The concern in Rosie's blue eyes turned to relief upon seeing us, and her lips curled into a welcoming smile. With her perfectly coifed short white hair, rosy cheeks, strand of pearls, and red festive apron covering her green dress, she looked like a 1950s holiday baking ad. Her boyfriend, Edmond, stood next to her, in a matching red apron dusted with flour covering his navy slacks and white oxford shirt. They eyed Gretta's disheveled look and candy-coated costume.

"Don't ask," Gretta snapped, blowing past the couple and into the house.

Rosie glared at Gretta's back, her smile tightening.

"Something smells delicious," I said.

Rosie's features softened and she led us inside, where the aroma of fresh-baked goods and Dean Martin's "A Marshmallow World" filled the air. The tension in my back eased for the first time since Gretta had announced receipt of her DNA results. Edmond slipped an arm around Rosie's waist and whirled her into the sitting room, with gray furnishings and light-blue walls. Garland and family photos decorated the top of an old piano and fireplace mantel. White twinkle lights and a lifetime collection of ornaments filled the branches of a towering spruce tree in the corner. At home three lonely ornaments hung on my artificial tree. I had serious ornament envy.

I handed Rosie the jar of whole nutmeg. "We were lucky to get the last one. You wouldn't believe—"

"Story for another time," Gretta said. "We should be off. Loads to do before the holiday."

Annoyance flashed in Rosie's eyes, but she managed a cheerful smile. "Wouldn't you fancy some tea and fresh-baked biscuits after the day you've apparently had?"

"Tea sounds wonderful." I shot Gretta a stern look.

The woman's determined expression relaxed slightly. "A quick cuppa would be grand."

Edmond looped an arm through Rosie's and whisked her out of the room before Gretta sucked the holiday spirit out of her.

At Halloween, Edmond and the two women had helped Biddy and me solve the mystery behind the skeleton we'd uncovered on the estate of Kiernan Moffat, a *Rags to Riches Roadshow* appraiser. Rosie had done her best to get along with Gretta and once commented about letting bygones be bygones. I wasn't sure what that meant.

Rosie returned with two plastic containers. She peeled back the corner of a lid, revealing unfrosted cookies in shapes of Christmas trees, snowmen, and reindeer.

Biddy and I gasped in awe, as if we'd just spotted Rudolph guiding Santa's sleigh over Ballycaffey.

"I know you said you would take care of the biscuits, but I thought you might have a difficult time finding unfrosted ones."

"Ah, that's brilliant, isn't it, now?" Biddy said.

I took the container. "Thanks so much."

Rosie removed the lid from a container with perky gingerbread men and women decorated with white icing and red candy dots.

Gretta stood paralyzed, the color draining from her face. Biddy stifled a distressed squeak. My breathing quickened, visions of Gretta taking out the gingerbread castle flashing through my head.

"Don't fancy gingerbread?" Rosie asked.

Gretta cleared her throat and regained her composure. She recounted our debacle in a nutshell and asked if Rosie might have time to create a three-foot gingerbread replica of Malahide Castle.

Rosie chuckled, then her gaze narrowed on Gretta's serious expression. "I'm preparing to host a holiday dinner. I don't have time to be making a gingerbread *bird*house, let alone a castle."

This was the first big dinner Rosie had made since her son, Sean, died five years ago and her late-husband Patrick two years later.

Gretta shrugged. "Just thought you might be wanting to help out a friend like I was helping you out getting the last jar of whole nutmeg for your pudding."

Rosie pressed her lips into a thin line, clutching her pearl necklace. Edmond returned with a cheerful smile and announced tea was almost ready.

"Sorry," I said. "We should be going after all. It's been a rough day." I practically pushed Gretta out the door before Rosie strangled the woman with her strand of pearls.

Rosie took a deep breath and eased it out.

"Are we still on for the cemetery visit in the morning?" Edmond asked.

I nodded. It was nearly Christmas, and I hadn't yet decorated my grandparents' graves. The first anniversary of Grandma's death had been rough on Edmond also, so I'd asked him to join me. He'd been sweet on Grandma. Hopefully, it would cheer us both up.

"Did you learn if Ian has any allergies or dietary restrictions?" Rosie asked.

"He doesn't."

I needed to inquire about my Murray family health history.

"My son was deathly allergic to nuts. It became his excuse for refusing to eat anything he disliked. 'I think I might be allergic to peas, mum. Whenever I eat the yokes, it feels like my tongue is swelling up.'" Rosie smiled reminiscently. "He had such a wit about him. And my Patrick was lactose intolerant. Made Christmas baking a wee bit of a challenge."

My dietary restrictions included no lamb. The first time I'd met Rosie, she'd served Biddy and me lamb for dinner. I'd discreetly slipped my meat onto Biddy's plate. Now that we were friends, Rosie knew I disliked it.

"I miss the hustle and bustle of preparing Christmas dinner for the family. Will be nice having the house full of loved ones again." Rosie teared up.

The car horn blared in the drive.

Biddy growled and bolted outside.

Rosie glared at the door, the moisture in her eyes evaporating. "I've done my best to get on with that woman. She makes it very difficult at times."

I nodded in agreement and gave Rosie a sympathetic hug, unable to share the reason behind Gretta's rude behavior. Gretta hadn't told anyone about the DNA test, not even her husband, Tommy, or daughter, Maeve. She'd forbidden me to confide in Biddy. Not having Maeve's blessing before taking the test made me even more nervous. As did discovering the identity of the baby's father, who was rumored to have been a local married man. Not only could Gretta's test be changing her family's lives forever, but possibly a married man's and the residents in Ballycaffey's close-knit community.

Colorful twinkle lights wrapped around the spindles on the iron fence in front of my yellow house, the former Ballycaffey National School. Before Biddy even parked on the blacktop drive, Gretta hopped out, her pillow tummy bouncing as she scurried toward the green front door.

"What is with her?" Biddy muttered, slamming the car door.

Gretta screeched to a halt, her gaze darting to Biddy. "Thought you were meeting your lad for dinner?"

"Not for a few hours. I'm coming in for a glass of mulled wine and biscuits." Biddy held up the plastic container of shortbread cookies in her hand.

Gretta shot me a distressed look.

Biddy eyed Gretta. "Why can't I be coming in?"

"Um, we can't eat any of those cookies," I said. "Need extras in case we screw up the frosting."

Biddy slid a suspicious gaze between Gretta and me. "Well, isn't this just grand. *Now* what are you two doing behind my back?"

I'd nearly slipped up several times and told Biddy about Gretta's quest to locate her grandson. Biddy knew I was keeping a secret from her.

Gretta and I remained silent.

Biddy thrust the container of cookies into my hands. "Fine." Wearing a hurt expression, she spun around and marched toward her car, the bells jingling on her elf booties.

"Wait," Gretta called out.

Biddy stopped, her back to us.

Gretta walked over to her. "If I be telling you this, you have to swear not to say a word."

Biddy turned to Gretta. "Of course I'd be keeping my gob shut."

"Not even Tommy knows about it."

Concern wrinkled Biddy's brow. "I promise."

"I took a DNA test to find the child Maeve put up for adoption."

A bright smile lit Biddy's face. "Ah, that's brilliant, isn't it now?" She hugged Gretta.

"I hope so," Gretta said. "The results just came in."

Biddy's eyes widened. "Then why are we standing here? Let's get crackin'." She linked an arm with Gretta's, and they rushed toward the door.

A nervous feeling tossed my stomach as I headed inside, where the earthy scent of peat and pine mingled in the cool air. The pine aroma was thanks to a candle.

The artificial tree's three ornaments included a replica of the Alaskan cruise ship I waitressed on one summer—a flaming baked Alaska had singed off a sliver of my eyebrow. A yellow foam wedge of cheese that read *Curd Nerd* from my two-month quest to find the tastiest deep-fried cheese curds at Wisconsin restaurants and fairs. In the end I'd gained five pounds and was featured in the newspaper that had organized the contest. And Abraham Lincoln's face carved in stone hung from a red ribbon weighting down several branches. I'd worked at a snack bar at Mount Rushmore one fall.

Growing up, it took our family of five three hours to decorate the tree with lights, garland, and over two hundred ornaments. At age twelve, I spent my first Christmas with Grandma. We'd strung white twinkle lights across the rose trellis outside the living room in place of a tree. A tradition I'd carried on. Grandma would have approved of my first Christmas tree, except for the lack of ornaments.

Gretta paced impatiently across the wood floor while I stacked peat logs and kindling in the green cast-iron stove tucked into a brick fireplace.

"Where's your computer?" she asked.

"In my office."

The woman hiked up her velvet dress and zipped up the spiral staircase. She returned moments later with my laptop.

I lit the fire, and heat warmed my cheeks even as a chill slithered up my spine, prickling the hairs on the back of my neck. I sank down into an overstuffed red couch cushion with my laptop. I tried to remain optimistic that if Gretta's grandson was a match, everything would work out dandy. Biddy sat on one side of me, Gretta on the other. Both of them nibbled on an unfrosted cookie while I logged into Gretta's DNA account.

Her closest match was an M.R. Pringle, male, aged thirty to thirty-nine. No location or family tree were provided. He'd established the account two years ago and logged in last week.

Gretta sucked in an excited gasp along with a bite of cookie. She coughed down the cookie and grasped my arm with a trembling hand. "That Pringle lad shares a load of DNA. He must be my grandson."

Biddy let out an excited squeal. "Ya found him!"

I didn't wish to burst my naïve friends' DNA bubble, but we shouldn't get our hopes up. Like I often did.

"Sharing 1,932 cM he could also be your half sibling or a half nephew." According to Gretta's sparse family tree, she didn't have a *known* full or half sibling, so no nephews either. "Can't imagine he's an uncle at his age. Yet anything is possible. If he *is* your grandson, he'd be a shared match with Tommy's relations, which aren't visible to you. Do you know if any Lynches have taken a DNA test?"

Gretta nibbled on a ragged fingernail she'd likely been gnawing on for six weeks. "Tommy's second cousin Martin and his siblings took the test to prove which of them is more

Irish. But if I contact him and he tells Tommy..." More fingernail nibbling. "I need to think on that."

"Speaking of being Irish," Biddy said. "This fella's ninety percent Irish and ten percent *Italian*. Interesting combination."

"Italian must come from the lad's father's side," Gretta said. "There's definitely no Italian in Tommy or my lines."

Never say never.

However, Gretta's estimated ethnicities were 95 percent Irish and 5 percent Scottish.

"Wonder if Pringle is the fella's last name or it's because he fancies the crisps," Biddy mused. "Like Mags's profile name could be Ms. Tayto."

Though obsessed as I was with the potato chips, my profile name was Margaret Catherine Murray. I was named after Grandma.

I researched the surname Pringle online. "It's Scottish. Originated centuries ago in Roxburghshire, a southern county that borders England."

Gretta nodded. "That makes sense. The couple who adopted the baby likely lived in England. At that time anyway. I'd sent Maeve to live with Tommy's cousin there until after the baby was born." She bit down on her quivering bottom lip, a look of regret in her eyes.

"I wonder if *M.R.* is for *mister* or his first and middle initials," I said.

"Your next closest match is a Birdie," Biddy said. "I've considered going by the nickname Birdie rather than Biddy. Know her, do ya?"

Gretta glared at the screen. "Unfortunately, but her

name's not Birdie—it's Mildred. Always went by Millie when I knew her."

"Then why does she be going by Birdie? Because she's mad about birds?"

"The woman has never cared about a thing besides herself."

According to Birdie's profile, she was over sixty years old and lived in County Galway. Her black-and-white profile picture was of a teenage girl with long hair pulled up in a bow. "A first cousin, I'm guessing, based on her age and the amount of shared DNA. Shares more than the average first cousin."

"Humph," Gretta grunted. "Just my luck." She bit the head off a snowman cookie.

Biddy and I exchanged curious glances.

"Is she related on your maternal or paternal side?" I asked.

"My mother's."

I checked Gretta and Birdie's shared matches, and the Pringle guy was at the top. "M.R. Pringle is a maternal connection."

"Millie's a nosey old bat. Would be surprised if she hasn't contacted him." Gretta's cheeks reddened. "Doesn't that just figure. The wretched woman communicated with my grandson before I did. And didn't even contact me to let me know she'd found him." She shoved the rest of the cookie into her mouth.

"What a right eejit," Biddy said.

"We don't know if she's had any contact with him," I said. "She might not be savvy enough to have determined their connection. Let's not jump to conclusions. And even if this M.R. Pringle is your grandson, he could be Ian's or Rory's son. Even Richard's."

A calm look washed over Gretta at the mention of her sons. "Wouldn't mind the lad being Richard's son. Would be a blessing still having a connection to him."

Richard had died in 1989. Ian farmed locally, and Rory worked nearby in real estate. None of them had ever been married or had any *known* children.

Gretta glared at Birdie's profile. "Trollop, skank..." She muttered a slew of nasty names.

"Ancestry.com doesn't disclose how a match is related to your shared matches or their amount of shared DNA," I said. "Most other test sites do. Those also show the chromosomes you match on, which is helpful. One of them even allows you to see your match's connections that you *don't* have in common. That could prove helpful in identifying this guy. With any luck, your cousin and M.R. Pringle are on other sites and one of them will have additional info on him."

Gretta looked hopeful.

"Janey," Biddy said. "You might know your relationship tomorrow."

"I doubt it'll be that easy." I turned to Gretta. "You're possibly going to need to contact Birdie, a Lynch relation, or M.R. Pringle to move forward with research."

A panicked look seized Gretta. "I can't be messaging the lad. What if I say the wrong thing and upset him? This is the type of news that should be delivered properly, in person. Says he logged into his account last week. Hopefully we can determine his relationship before he signs on again and messages me." She squeezed my arm. "You need to change my name and location so he can't track me down. Not yet." Her gaze darted around frantically, landing on her costume. "Change it to Mrs. Claus."

"How about your initials? Mrs. Claus might sound too cheery and approachable when you're not wanting to be contacted."

"Maybe I should be hiding my account."

"You can only see your matches, if they can see you. And even if you hide a match from your list, you'll still appear on that person's list."

"Let's do my initials."

Before Gretta and Biddy left, I became a collaborator for Gretta's DNA account, allowing me access to her matches while using my account's research subscription. And I downloaded her raw DNA file to my laptop.

I was set to go.

I reached for another cookie, noticing we'd polished off a quarter of them. I put the lid on the container, my yellow wellies on my feet, and headed out to the woodshed. I stuck the container on a shelf with gardening tools. I filled a burlap bag with peat and headed back inside. I only trudged through the long grass to the shed when I was down to my last piece of peat. The cookies should be safe there.

I checked the status of Dad's and Ian's golf balls. The package was on schedule for delivery tomorrow. I poured a celebratory glass of wine and grabbed a bag of Taytos from the cupboard before settling in with my laptop on the couch in front of a roaring fire.

After uploading Gretta's DNA to other sites, I scanned her matches on Ancestry.com. Besides Gretta's two closest matches, M.R. Pringle and Birdie, the rest were extended family and distant relations. That made sense. Gretta was an only child. As far as she knew anyway. Her mother had one sister, and the only thing she knew about her father was his name and death date. He'd died young. How sad to have no family history. A few distant matches shared her mother's uncommon surname Mulkerrin. Surprisingly, only a handful had her dad's popular last name Kelly.

The other sites' results might be available tomorrow.

I wouldn't be getting much sleep tonight...or possibly until New Year's.

# Three

~

PINKY WAS outside the kitchen window, gobbling up Froot Loops off the grass while I enjoyed the same late breakfast in a bowl at the table. The large sheep with a bright-pink splash of dye on his wool hung out in my yard more than his owner's field. Surrounded by perky yellow walls, I was singing along to "Feliz Navidad" despite not knowing the Spanish lyrics. I added lasagna, my family's traditional Christmas Eve meal, to my grocery list. Christmas day Mom had made ham with a pineapple glaze. I had Dad's favorite cereal, soda, and peanut butter on the list. I had no clue about Ian's favorite foods. At the Murray reunion, he'd recommended several craft beers to Dad. I had to have more than beer on hand for him.

I finished off my second cup of tea, trying to work up the energy to start cleaning after a restless sleep. Dad was staying in my upstairs bedroom, and Ian in the master bedroom off the living room. Vacuuming the cobwebs was number one on my to-do list. At least the ones on the ceiling that were visible when lying in bed. I just wouldn't look at the ceiling when I was sleeping on the couch.

I checked, and Gretta's DNA matches hadn't yet materialized on the other sites. A sense of relief washed over me. With any luck the results wouldn't post until after the holiday.

An email popped into my inbox notifying me that the golf balls had been delivered. I sprang from my chair and raced to the front door. No package on the stoop, I zipped through the conservatory and out back. Nothing on the wooden patio. Baffled, I pulled up the tracking information, including a photo of a small brown box on a red doormat partially covering a gray concrete porch. My welcome mat was green, my stoop plain boring cement. Great. I'd even included my Eircode to *ensure* a seamless delivery. Not merely National Schoolhouse, Ballycaffey, County Westmeath. Not even a sliver of a door or house was visible to help identify where the package had been misdelivered.

I shoved my feet into the yellow wellies and my arms into a green wool coat and stomped out to my car. I cruised up and down every nearby road searching for my package. A half hour later, I hadn't found the box or a gray porch with a red mat. I stopped at McCarthy's pub hoping someone might recognize the porch.

Biddy was at work. Her parents, Ita and Daniel, owned the pub and stood behind the bar decorated with garland and twinkle lights. Dressed in a lime-green sweater and jeans, Ita's blond hair was styled in a chin-length bob with a few green highlights. She was a hairdresser, yet the colored streaks were adventurous for her. My chestnut-colored hair tossed up in a clip was boring in comparison. New Year's would be the perfect time for a new style.

Daniel pushed up the sleeves of his blue plaid button-up shirt, preparing to replenish drinks for the crowd watching the dart tournament. Spotting me, his blue eyes sparkled, and he gave me a wave. "What's the craic, Maggie Mae?"

Daniel had given me that nickname years ago. A much better one than Tombstone Terminator, given to me by the two short stocky men with receding gray hairlines, engrossed in the dart championship on TV. I'd nicknamed them John Deere and Beckham. The one with a bit of a belly always wore the tractor company's T-shirts, and the other soccer jerseys. Johnny's shirt had a red Santa's cap hanging from the deer's antlers.

I told Biddy's parents about my misdelivered package, but neither of them recognized the porch.

"Best wait for a break in the match before showing the snap around, or ya mightn't be getting their full attention," Daniel said.

I dropped down onto a stool and snatched two foil-covered chocolates from a bowl on the bar. I unwrapped one and popped it into my mouth, staring at the framed photo of a sheep on the wall over the register. The animal's back hooves on the floor, front ones on the bar, it was sniffing a pint of Guinness next to the toes of my pink tennies. I'd have won a gold medal for the high jump, springing from the floor up onto the bar. Someone had snapped a pic of that infamous day I was chased by a sheep.

Ita gave me a reassuring smile. "You'll find it. Even if you didn't, your dad and Ian wouldn't be caring about you not having pressies for them. They care about spending time with you."

I nodded. "It's just frustrating."

"At least it wasn't nicked," Ita said.

"Sadly, thieves don't take a holiday," Daniel said before welcoming two men entering the pub.

"Your cemetery restoration site looks brilliant." Ita relaxed her forearms on the bar. "Ian and his sister, Ava, did a lovely job decorating the castle's graves for the holidays. Their Twelve Days of Christmas snaps are gorgeous. Never know what they will be posting the next day. My favorite was the one of Ian climbing the tree to get the partridge down. I'm sure the bird was photoshopped in the tree, but still hilarious."

"Wait until you see the one with eight maids a-milking with Enid the cow's tombstone. The animal that produced sixteen calves and loads of milk." Ian, the Dalwade Castle Hotel owner Archie, and six local men had dressed as milking maids.

Ian and Ava had been real troopers executing my ideas for the festive photos. During the Clan Murray reunion at Dalwade Castle Hotel in Scotland, Dad and several relations had decided to invest in the medieval castle's refurbishments. I was in charge of the estate's cemetery restoration project. At the gathering, I'd also taken the lead in proving Ian was innocent of his brother Malcolm's murder. Discovering the identity of my biological father—as well as my nasty uncle Malcolm with an arrow in his chest—had caused more drama than your average family reunion.

"Trying to keep the momentum going until the *Rags to Riches Roadshow* films there in April. Last month's appearance on those ghost hunters' video helped spike sales through the end of the year, anyway." Thanks to Biddy tripping over a buried headstone and uncovering an unknown grave. And the silly ghost hunters had thought they needed to tell *us* how to add excitement and drama to a reality show. Our lives were one big reality show. "January and February are slow months. We need to keep coming up with promo ideas besides discounted cabin-fever rates."

Ita peered over at her husband, chatting about darts. "I'll help fill up a few nights in January. Daniel and I could use a romantic getaway. I'd love to pay Euphemia's grave a visit."

Ita had adopted the servant's grave. A local volunteer caretaker and up to five others could adopt the grave to pay for its upkeep.

I smiled. "Thanks. That'd be great. I don't recommend Euphemia's Quarters, since it has twin beds."

Biddy and I had stayed in the former servant's room where Lord Kerr supposedly impregnated the poor woman, who bore his only son. She became his wife after his first wife suspiciously died. I doubted the average servant had a top-floor room with an incredible view. Actually, it'd had a view of the tower's stone defensive wall until we'd climbed out the window onto the tower to enjoy the scenic surroundings.

"Wait here," Ita said. She walked through the door behind the bar into the family's residence. She returned with a small crystal snowman wearing a red Santa's cap with a green ribbon strung through it. "Your mum gave me a set of three of them the first Christmas I was married. Each one has a different color cap. I'd like you to have one."

Ita and my mom had been best friends and classmates until my parents had married and Mom left Ireland. Mom didn't return often, and the women had grown apart, whereas Biddy and I'd grown closer. I'd visited Grandma every chance I had.

I teared up. "Thank you. Biddy told you about my pathetic tree, didn't she?"

Ita nodded, reaching across the bar and giving my hand a gentle squeeze. "But that's not the reason I want you to have it."

I wiped away a tear as John Deere and Beckham walked over to the bar and ordered a pizza. I showed them the photo, hoping they'd recognize the porch.

Beckham shook his head in disgust. "Hope it wasn't nicked while sitting on that porch. Heard thieves have been following around the delivery vans."

"Ya should be installing some of them security cameras on the door," John Deere said.

Wouldn't do me much good in this case since the package was misdelivered, but something to think about.

He shook a finger at the photo. "Right, then, me friend Morris laid that concrete for David Griffin." He gave me directions to a house located nowhere near mine.

I thanked the man, gave Ita and Daniel a wave goodbye, and headed out the door, nearly slamming into Biddy's boyfriend, Collin—a cute brown-haired guy dressed in tan slacks and a blue wool jacket.

Collin smiled. "What's the craic, Mags? Saw your car. Do you have a sec?"

"Sure."

He gave Ita a wave behind the bar. "Outside."

That sounded serious.

We stepped outside, where a dozen cars lined the sides of

the narrow road. Collin shot a nervous glance around the side of the building toward the McCarthys' residence in back.

"Biddy's at work," I said. "What's up?"

"It's about her Christmas present." He peered over his shoulder. "I'm not taking her to a fancy hotel in Dublin."

"Why not?"

A nervous smile twitched the corners of his mouth. "I'm taking her to Paris."

My eyes widened. My jaw dropped. "Paris?"

He nodded excitedly. "A few months ago, a fella at work was mentioning his sister has a flat in Paris. She was needing someone to mind the place and her cat over New Year's. Don't be telling Biddy the house-minding part."

Wouldn't she be wondering why a cat was there?

"Not allergic to cats, is she?" he asked.

I shook my head.

"That's grand. Should only be one. The fella said the kittens should all have homes by New Year's. The only available restaurants are fierce expensive. Thought I'd be making her dinner. The kitchenette has a stove. Do you think not going out to some fancy place will upset her? Wondering now if I did the right thing not booking the Dublin package."

"I think you could dine at a hotdog stand and she'll be happy. Seriously. You're taking her to Paris. She's not going to care about the dinner."

A huge smile replaced the nervous look on Collin's face. "I was hoping you'd be saying that. Just bought a French phrase book. Thought she'll be surprised since I'm not the Paris kind of fella."

I nodded. "She'll be surprised. Are you giving her the book for Christmas? Like as a teaser?"

He shook his head. "Not telling her until I take the Dublin airport exit instead of heading into the city."

Oh man. Biddy wouldn't like *that* surprise. She'd want advance notice to go on a shopping spree. Packing for chic Paris wine bars and cafés was much different than packing for Dublin's pubs.

Collin's brow wrinkled. "What's wrong?"

"I think it's best to give her a heads-up so she can pack for Paris rather than Dublin."

"Maybe you could help her pack, knowing it's for Paris."

"If I pack Biddy's suitcase, she'll definitely know something is up."

"Paris will be mad crazy with the holiday, so I'm ordering sightseeing tickets in advance. What do you think she'll be wanting to do?"

"Let me think on that and I'll let you know."

"Thanks a mil, Mags. This has to be perfect." Collin hopped into his car and cruised down the narrow lane between parked cars.

I'd never seen the guy so nervous.

*This has to be perfect...*

Holy cats! Was Collin going to propose to Biddy?

They'd just started officially dating this past summer. And besides Collin not being a Paris kind of guy, I didn't picture him being a *married* kind of guy. At least not yet. Surely he was merely being a *sweet* guy taking Biddy to Paris. Speaking of sweets, Biddy better stock up on a few more boxes of his favorite candy.

Biddy was spending New Year's Eve in Paris, while I was

spending it at home—alone. Both Dad and Ian had to leave prior to the new year. I'd be devouring a pan of store-made lasagna unless I got adventurous and bought the ingredients for homemade lasagna. That would be my excitement for the evening. Actually, it'd be the perfect time to start reading the three-volume series the appraiser Kiernan Moffat had given me for solving the mystery of the skeleton on his estate. *Letters, Queen Victoria, 1837-1861.* The collection of Queen Victoria's letters covered a fascinating period from the time the young queen ascended the throne until she lost her dear Prince Albert. First edition, of course.

I headed to the Griffins' house located down a one-lane road with a strip of grass growing up the center. A blow-up Frosty the Snowman swayed in the wind in the white bungalow's yard. No car sat in the drive, but a red doormat sat on the gray porch. Nobody answered the door. I popped over to the neighbors. A middle-aged man in jeans and a blue wool sweater answered the door. I explained my situation.

"Griffins are gone for the holiday. We're collecting their deliveries and post. I just got in. Didn't see anything over there." He called out to his teenage son in the next room, who confirmed he hadn't collected a package either.

I thanked them and headed home. If Gretta was still on road-rubbish duty, part of her community service work for Finn's accident, she'd likely have spotted the thief. As if I needed one more mystery to solve.

If I didn't find the package, what was I going to get Dad and Ian only nine days before Christmas? Aunt Ava had given me the Murray family's secret recipe for Christmas pudding with eighteen ingredients, including grated nutmeg. Ava said Ian would be thrilled since he didn't bake—yet neither did I. Being a history professor, Ian was big into history. He played golf and was involved in Dalwade Castle's refurbishment project. Oh, and I'd learned at the reunion that he'd studied at the Sorbonne in Paris and spoke French. Last month I'd called him for the first time, and we'd chatted for nearly fifteen minutes. We had spoken a few times since, mainly about my genealogy work. A safe topic. Next call, I needed to learn more about his interests so I was better prepared for his birthday. If it was after the Murray reunion this past September, I missed it.

Upon arriving at home, I hung the crystal snowman on my little tree. It glistened against the sunlight streaming in through the back window. I missed our family tree-decorating traditions. The evening had kicked off with a spaghetti dinner and garlic bread. While Dad wrapped strands of large vintage bulbs around a pine tree in the corner of the living room, Mom, my sisters—Emma and Mia—and I hauled boxes of ornaments up from the basement. The first ornaments on the tree were Grandma Murray's crocheted snowflakes. Then I'd dig through the boxes for the reindeer painted on a red glass ball that I'd made in art class. I smiled at the crystal snowman, envisioning Mom picking out the perfect gift for her best friend and Ita opening it.

I didn't have a gift for Biddy!

I'd been so focused on getting Dad's and Ian's gifts I'd totally zoned about one for Biddy. I'd get her a gorgeous blouse or something chic for her Paris trip. I went to her favorite shop online and found a purple blouse and vintage-looking dangly earrings. Perfect for Paris!

I posted the theft to the Ballycaffey Action Group on social media, warning locals about a package thief on the loose. I asked if anyone else had been a victim of a theft. Next, I called the delivery company. The representative offered to refund the package if it wasn't found in seventy-two hours. Great, yet that didn't solve the issue of not having gifts for Dad and Ian. The golf ball company estimated a replacement order wouldn't arrive until after New Year's. I needed a backup gift.

The doorbell rang.

I opened the door, and a frazzled Gretta flew inside.

"When I dropped off a few dozen toys at the grocery store, the manager informed me that the baker's livid about his masterpiece being demolished over a jar of nutmeg." She paced the living room floor, tossing her arms in the air. "He said he hadn't time to recreate it. After I got home, she rang and said in the spirit of Christmas and the children's toy drive, he'd do it if he's able to find assistants. Could build a bloody castle for what he quoted to create the gingerbread one, but I haven't a choice. Can't be letting everyone down, and I need karma back on my side."

"I'm sure he'll come through."

"Won't be done till New Year's, but better than not at all." Gretta shook off her frustration. "Any leads on my Mr. Pringle?"

"Last I checked, the other sites hadn't loaded. I can look again." I sat at the kitchen table in front of my laptop and soggy bowl of Froot Loops. Gretta impatiently drummed her fingers against the table while I checked the sites.

I shook my head. "Nothing yet."

She collapsed back onto the chair. "Need to be learning if the lad is a Lynch. Will have to tell Tommy so I can contact his cousin Martin."

"I think telling Tommy is a good idea. Better to let him know you're searching for your grandson before you've found him. The GenDNA results will show your unrelated matches. Most will be distant relations with initials or random aliases for their profile names."

"Would you come with me to tell Tommy?"

The last thing I wanted was to be put in the middle of more family drama. I had enough of my own. Actually, not a lot lately since my sisters had me on ignore status for nearly a year. Since I'd inherited Grandma's house and decided not to sell it and graciously split my share with them.

Fifteen minutes later, Gretta and I were sitting in her daffodil-yellow living room on a cream-colored couch. Her husband, Tommy, a gray-haired man with a bit of a belly, sat in a matching chair next to a roaring fire in a woodstove tucked into a white marble fireplace. Once again I was suffering from ornament envy, admiring the tall artificial tree in the corner. Especially the carved wooden characters from *The Nutcracker* ballet, including Clara and the Mouse King.

After a bit of awkward chitchat, suspicion flickered in Tommy's happy brown eyes. Gretta took the plunge and confessed about her DNA test.

Tommy's gaze darkened. "Six weeks ago ya took the test and are just now telling me about it?" His gaze darted to me.

I swallowed hard. He likely assumed the test had been my idea.

He turned to Gretta, and I let out a relieved sigh. "Should have been making this decision together, we should've."

"You'd have insisted I not take the test."

"Damn straight I would have." Tommy's head reddened

beneath his thinning gray hair. "If Maeve finds out, I'll never see her again. You're not destroying my relationship with our daughter. I won't have it." He pounded a fist against the chair's arm. "I won't."

My palms started sweating.

Gretta bolted upright on the couch. "Where were you thirty-one years ago when I was dealing with Maeve's pregnancy? You didn't argue for her to keep the child then. You didn't speak out on her behalf."

Tommy looked taken aback by Gretta's defensive attitude. "Aye, precisely why I'm doing it now, it is. You need to stop looking for him."

"I can't," Gretta said. "I'm sorry. I have to do this."

"No ya don't. Ya have a choice, ya do. Just like ya had a choice about insisting Maeve give up her baby. It's a choice you're gonna have to live with."

"I can't," Gretta muttered, her shoulders drooping.

Tommy shook a stern finger at his wife. "When she's home for New Year's, you'll be telling her what you've done." He stabbed a thumb in his chest. "*I'll* be telling her I had no part in it. And ya won't be contacting the lad until Maeve knows what's going on. Promise me that, or I swear I'll be ringing her and telling her meself!"

Gretta nodded faintly.

Tommy stormed from the room. The front door slammed shut, and moments later his truck roared to life. The vehicle's engine quickly faded in the distance. Gretta and I collapsed back against the couch.

His reaction would undoubtedly be calm compared to Maeve's when she learned about Gretta's test. However, if Gretta hadn't taken the test, it was only a matter of time before one of Maeve's brothers or other relations took one, with its popularity on the rise in Ireland. I wouldn't blame Maeve for being furious about the test when Gretta had insisted her child be put up for adoption. However, Maeve had been eighteen. Legally, she could have chosen to keep her baby. Yet not having her family's support would have made it difficult. It wasn't my place to judge.

Gretta stood. "I'll be ringing Martin Lynch."

"Are you sure that's a good idea? Tommy will be even more upset if he learns you called his cousin."

Gretta shrugged. "He never talks to the man. Besides, that can't be helped. He'll get over it."

I wasn't so sure about that.

"I knew I'd have to be telling Maeve at some point. Besides, if Martin isn't a match with Mr. Pringle, then I'll tell Tommy he's not our grandson. No need to say anything to Maeve. Not unless the lad does one day appear as a match."

I doubted Tommy was going to go for that.

"And if he's not my grandson, I don't care to know who he is or how he's related."

That sounded good to me.

Gretta left the room and returned with her address book and phone.

"We need a game plan before calling him," I said. "If you tell him you and M.R. Pringle are a match, it'll be obvious the guy is descended from Tommy and you. And you can't tell him Tommy took the test because he'd wonder why Tommy isn't showing up under his matches." I pondered the best course of action. "You could say a distant relation contacted you wondering if Tommy had taken a test under an anonymous name and matched an M.R. Pringle. Seeing as

Tommy hasn't taken one, in the Christmas spirit, you offered to check with his relations."

Gretta nodded enthusiastically. "That's a good one."

She called Martin who was tending to cattle. He promised to call her back in an hour.

I stood and grabbed my green wool coat from the back of a rocking chair. "Stop over after you hear from him."

"He said it'd be within the hour." Gretta's gaze pleaded me to stay. "He's on his way home soon, and his wife will know his account information."

I didn't want to be here when Tommy returned. Yet it might be a few days before he cooled down and came home. I tossed my jacket back on the chair and admired the tree's ornaments again.

Gretta removed a reindeer one made from popsicle sticks hanging from a red ribbon. "Maeve made this when she was young." She brushed a finger over the deer's googly plastic eyes. "She wasn't mature enough to have a child. She refused to mind other peoples' children for extra spending money. She had no patience for wee ones. She had no patience for *anyone*. She thought my not wanting her to keep the child was all about appearances, but that wasn't the case. I'd raised my children. I didn't want to raise a grandchild." She frowned. "That sounds awful now."

I shook my head. "No, it doesn't."

A half hour later the phone rang. Gretta and I shared nervous glances. My heart raced as she answered Martin's call. Gretta barely uttered a word during the conversation. She wished Tommy's cousin a happy holiday and hung up.

She peered over at me. "He and Mr. Pringle share 67 cM."

"That means the Pringle guy is likely his second cousin twice removed." My heart thumped against my chest. "I'd say he's your grandson."

A smile curled the corners of Gretta's thin lips, and her eyes watered.

"Remember, he could be a son's child. Also keep in mind that your grandson might merely have taken the DNA test to determine his ethnicity estimates. His adoption might have come as a shock. He established an Ancestry.com account two years ago, but he may have taken the test recently. The fact that his DNA account is still activated is a positive sign."

When people discovered a DNA surprise, they often logged off their account and never returned.

Hopefully, that wouldn't be the case with M.R. Pringle.

I went home to clean. Before hauling the vacuum up the spiral staircase to my bedroom, I checked my computer and discovered Gretta's DNA had loaded to two sites. Drumming my fingers nervously against the keyboard, I twisted my mouth in contemplation. Would I sleep better if I did or didn't review her matches? Curiosity won.

Her cousin Birdie wasn't on either site. Gretta's closest match on the third-party site GenDNA was Casper. DNA results from all test companies could be uploaded to this one site. Casper and M.R. Pringle had both uploaded their DNA from Ancestry.com. Both men also shared almost the same amount of DNA with Gretta and many of the same matches between the two sites.

M.R. Pringle and Casper were undoubtedly the same person.

People sometimes used different profile names on the various sites. Why Casper? *Casper* (the friendly ghost) was his favorite movie? Like Casper, the guy wanted to remain a ghost until he was ready to identify himself? He lived in Casper, Wyoming?

Casper didn't have a family tree, and his email address provided no identifying clues, such as his country code. I searched his email online, and nothing popped up. The site required an email address, so people often created one just for that profile's correspondence. I was tempted to send the person a vague message that I was a genealogist managing a client's account. However, besides fearing the wrath of Tommy, I couldn't go against his request that Gretta didn't contact their grandson before telling Maeve.

Speaking of Gretta, I shot her an email about Casper.

The top thousand matches Gretta and the guy *didn't* share in common were distant ones, none with the surname Lynch. No names jumped out at me for potential local father candidates. However, it could be mother candidates I was looking for if the child was one of Gretta's son's and not Maeve's.

We now knew M.R. Pringle slash Casper was a Lynch.

Descended from *which* Lynch sibling was the question.

## Four

THE NEXT MORNING Biddy and I sat at my kitchen table decorating Rosie's cutout cookies with red, green, and white frosting and colorful sprinkles. We were eating spoonfuls of lemon frosting—our backup when we initially couldn't find white. I filled her in on Gretta's Casper match, and between frosting each cookie, I searched the internet for replacement gifts for Dad and Ian.

Finally warmed up, Biddy shrugged off her favorite green fleece rugby jacket, which she'd worn over a red sweater with snowflakes. She always dressed for the holidays, even when working at the hospital's pediatric ward. My favorite was her green-and-red nurse's uniform with Snoopy dressed as Santa, and Woodstock as an elf.

"You could have the likeness of them made into bobble-heads dressed in Murray tartan kilts and matching caps, holding golf clubs," Biddy said. "My uncle Seamus has a bobblehead collection. Hundreds of the yokes. Most are celebrities like Father Ted or sports figures. He gives me one from his collection every birthday and Christmas. Not sure if it's an early inheritance or I look like a bobblehead fan. I'm expecting Ringo, this year seeing as I already have John, Paul, and George."

"I don't think customized gifts are a good idea at this point. They wouldn't make it here in time."

"Buy plain golf balls and have an artist paint their initials on them."

That was a better idea than the bobbleheads.

Biddy admired her green frosted Christmas tree cookie with colorful candy ornaments, which had taken her a half hour to decorate. "A true masterpiece. Could be putting a string through the top of a few and glazing them. Make ornaments and give them to your dad and Ian as gifts."

"I made ornaments for my parents in third-grade art class."

"But you never did it for Ian. And your artistic skills have certainly improved. Could also be using a few more ornaments for your tree. Most shops have them fifty percent off at this point."

"I don't want to decorate the tree with a box of glass balls that cost five euros. I want ornaments to have meaning. Like the cute crystal snowman from your mom. Thanks to you, I'm guessing."

Biddy shrugged off a guilty grin. "Your biscuits are lovely."

Distracted while looking for gifts, I'd frosted over an already decorated tree and drawn a snowman's face on the bottom snowball.

"I might end up giving Collin cookie ornaments or part of my bobblehead collection if I don't come up with a gift idea."

"What about a romantic weekend at Dalwade Castle?"

Biddy shook her head. "My mum told me she's surprising my dad with a weekend there. I can't be giving the same gift to Collin. Besides, even with our discount, that's a bit dear and might come across as too romantic."

*Collin is taking you to Paris!*

The doorbell echoed frantically through the house.

"Maybe someone on the action group found your stolen gift," Biddy said.

I raced to the front door, where Gretta's nose was pressed up against the small glass window, a panicked look in her gray eyes. I let her in, and she blew past me into the living room, where Biddy stood with a spoonful of lemon frosting and her Christmas tree cookie.

"What's wrong?" Biddy asked. "The baker refuse to make the gingerbread castle?"

Gretta shook her head. "Even worse. The garda rang and wants to meet with me. That store manager promised not to be pressing charges as long as I could replace the castle. The baker must not have found a team. So much for her holiday spirit. I can't be spending the holiday in jail." The woman's gaze darted desperately around the house. "You have to be hiding me."

"He can't be arresting ya before Christmas," Biddy said.

"Can't be arresting me afterward either," Gretta snapped.

"Did he say he's coming to arrest you?" I asked.

"What else could he have been ringing about?"

"He didn't tell you why he was calling?"

"I panicked and hung up on him."

"Ya should have been asking," Biddy said. "Maybe one of those road cameras caught ya speeding."

"I think he'd be popping a speeding ticket in the mail," I said. "Hand delivering tickets would be a full-time job."

"No worries," Biddy told Gretta. "If the officer wants to talk to you about the castle, we'll hire a baker from Dublin if we have to."

I nodded. "It'll all work out. It's the season of perpetual hope."

"Suppose I can be ringing him back and agree to meet. Called an hour ago. I was on the motorway heading for Cork when I decided fleeing probably wasn't the best idea."

Like the time she'd fled the scene of the crime after accidentally running Finn O'Brien off the road.

The doorbell rang.

"This has to be your golf balls," Biddy said. "Maybe the delivery fella was able to recover them."

Rather than a guy dressed in slacks and a logoed delivery jacket, a gorgeous dark-haired guy around my age—twenty-seven—dressed in a black suit and purple tie peered through the door's window. I darted out of view and smoothed a hand over my hair and wiped any cookie crumbs or frosting from my mouth.

I opened the door, greeting him with a smile.

"I'm wondering if Gretta Lynch might be here. Called in at her house—nobody was home. Someone at the pub up the road mentioned I might be finding her here. I'm Detective Brennan."

My heart raced. He was there to arrest Gretta, not to see me. Besides, after my twenty-four-hour engagement to Josh, followed by Finn, I'd pledged never to fall for a guy merely because of his good looks. I ushered the man into the living room, where Biddy stood licking lemon frosting from the spoon.

Gretta had vanished.

"You can't be arresting a person on the holidays." Biddy shook her spoon at the man, and a yellow glob of frosting flew through the air and landed on the lapel of his black suit jacket.

He eyed his jacket, then shot Biddy an annoyed glance.

"Ah, sorry about that." She plucked the frosting from his jacket and stuck it back on the spoon. "Anyway, we'll find someone to bake the bloody yoke."

The guy's blue-eyed gaze narrowed in confusion. "Are you Gretta Lynch?"

Biddy shook her head. "But I witnessed what happened. In all fairness to Gretta, that other woman was as much at fault, trying to snatch the jar away from her."

"Right, then." He smoothed a hand down his tie. "I think there's some confusion. I'd like to speak to Mrs. Lynch about her recent DNA test."

How did the detective know Gretta had taken a DNA test?

Unless he was a match. Or a match of a match on GenDNA. Or...a law enforcement officer who'd uploaded a criminal's DNA to that database searching for relations to help solve a case. That was quick. Her test had just loaded to the site yesterday. It had to be a serious crime if authorities were monitoring the person's profile so closely.

"What about her test?" I asked calmly, my heart racing.

"I'm not allowed to divulge that information to anyone but Mrs. Lynch."

I squared my shoulders. "I'm her genealogist." Hopefully, she wasn't in need of a lawyer more than a family historian.

The guy looked mildly intrigued. If he couldn't talk to Gretta, maybe I'd have to do. I couldn't speak on Gretta's behalf when it came to solving a criminal case.

"Gretta," I called out to the closed bedroom door.

The knotty-pine door slowly opened. Gretta shot me a perturbed glance and joined us in the living room.

"Is there a place we can speak in private?" the detective asked her.

Gretta squared her narrow shoulders. "I won't be talking to you without my genealogist in my presence."

He reluctantly agreed. "Your DNA was loaded to a third-party site and is a match with a suspect in an ongoing investigation."

Gretta gasped in awe. Having assisted me with solving several mysteries, helping the authorities solve a cold case would be a dream come true.

"How close of a match is it?" Usually the connection was so distant you didn't know the person.

The guy eyed Gretta. "Sure you wouldn't prefer to discuss this in private?"

"Quite sure. Who is this match?"

"That's what we'd like to know. He's your closest match. Profile name is Casper."

Gretta paled. Biddy chewed off the top of her award-worthy Christmas tree cookie. I bit down on my lower lip. The authorities had likely chosen Casper as a profile name because the man was a ghost in the wind.

"Your assistance could help solve a five-year-old case."

"What was the crime?" I asked.

"I'm not at liberty to divulge the details."

Biddy's gaze narrowed on the detective. "Then why should Gretta be divulging the details about her DNA match?"

"Because her cooperation will put a criminal in jail and prevent future crimes by this person. It's critical that we apprehend this man ASAP."

I'd feared Gretta's DNA test would reveal a family secret, not a criminal. Even though I'd often envisioned the day FBI agents would rap on my door and request my assistance in solving a cold case involving one of my DNA matches. As long as that match was a distant cousin I'd never heard of.

"I suppose I have no choice but to assist," Gretta said. "It's—"

I grasped the woman's arm. "Wait a minute." I peered over at the detective. "Last I knew, Irish law enforcement isn't permitted to use genealogy DNA sites to identify criminals due to privacy issues. Has that law changed?"

Irish citizens were allowed to download their DNA to GenDNA. However, a person had to opt in to authorize *US* law enforcement to view it. I shouldn't have opted Gretta in.

The detective's gaze dimmed, and his right eye twitched with irritation. "No. That's still the law. However, the NSU, Ireland's National Surveillance Unit, is assisting US authorities with the investigation. Based on DNA analysis, they determined the suspect is Irish but are unsure of his location."

"Still doesn't seem legal for the Irish police to be actively investigating such a case," I said.

He forced a smile. "I assure you it is."

"The match is my half sibling," Gretta blurted out. "My father had an affair with a young woman who minded me. She became pregnant and moved away. I haven't a clue what happened to her or her child, and I don't care to know. I'll be of no help in your investigation." Gretta's eyes watered. The corners of her mouth quivered. "I'm sorry. This brings up horrible memories I'd sooner forget. I'd merely taken the test to learn my ethnicities."

Gretta had fabricated that story awfully fast. Was there truth to the tale?

"My genealogist can vouch for the connection." Gretta turned to me. "Isn't that right?"

I nodded faintly, my palms sweating. I'd just lied to an officer about a criminal investigation. What if Gretta's grandson was a serial killer? If he killed more people and I'd withheld information that could have assisted in the guy's arrest, those murders were on me. What if they determined who the guy was and learned I'd lied? Could I go to prison even though it wasn't legal and the Irish police were skirting the law to assist US authorities with the case?

However, I didn't know the man's identity or location.

The detective's dreamy blue eyes stared into mine. "Sure about that connection, are you?"

"Casper has an Ancestry.com account. Why would the person willingly take a DNA test if he's a wanted criminal?" I asked, avoiding his question.

He shrugged, his eye once again twitching, growing more irritated with my questions. He hadn't been prepared for a *genealogist* to interrogate *him*.

"He likely hadn't realized his DNA was left at the scene," he said. "Most criminals think they're careful and above the law. And like you said, genetic genealogy isn't used in Ireland. Doubt the fella has a clue how it works."

Biddy nodded. "There are a lot of dumb criminals out there. Like that fella who robbed a bank in Wexford, then stole a car to escape, leaving his car parked in front of the bank." She glanced over at Gretta. "Not that your, er, half sibling is that dumb."

The detective slipped a business card from his suit jacket pocket and handed it to Gretta. "If you should change your mind and decide to help out your country, I'd appreciate you notifying me at the NSU."

I pointed a finger in the air. "Actually, wouldn't she be helping out the *United States*?"

He gave me a tight smile, looking ready to arrest me for annoying an officer. "She'd be helping the entire world. Who knows where his next crime will take place?" He turned and left.

"Fair play to ya." Biddy gave me a pat on the back. "Calling him out on the privacy law. He hadn't a clue what he was in for when he came here looking for Gretta. He thought he was going to scare us into giving up all sorts of details on that Casper fella."

I smiled proudly.

Gretta dropped down onto the couch, exhaling a shaky breath. "My grandson is a wanted killer," she muttered in disbelief.

"You don't know he's wanted for *murder*," Biddy said. "Maybe he's a drug dealer or bank robber."

I shot Biddy an incredulous look.

"I'm sure there's a legit reason why his DNA was at the

crime scene, and he likely had nothing to do with it," Biddy said.

Gretta nodded faintly. "You're right. He can't be guilty. We've never had a criminal in the family."

What about Gretta nearly killing Finn O'Brien, knocking me unconscious with her purse, and almost ending up in the slammer due to the gingerbread debacle?

"I need to stop searching for my grandson," Gretta said.

A sense of relief washed over me. I wouldn't have to tell Gretta that I was ethically torn about not having confessed to the detective that the match was her grandson rather than a half sibling. Or worry about keeping his name and whereabouts a secret. Now, I'd never know either. Yet Gretta would never get to know her grandson. Or if he was innocent or guilty.

"I refuse to help the police find him," she said. "What if they've already hacked into my DNA accounts or bugged my phone?" Her gaze darted around. "What if he bugged the room?" She raced over to where the detective had been standing next to the love seat and checked under the cushions and end table.

"I doubt it'd be easy, not to mention illegal, for them to hack into your ancestry account and bug my place."

Yet the Irish police were skirting the privacy law by helping the US authorities.

"Deactivate my accounts. I'm done looking for the lad."

Gretta marched out of the house.

"I still can't imagine a felon loading his DNA to a genealogy test site," I said. "Certainly not one that allows law enforcement access."

Biddy shrugged. "A lot of dumb felons."

I nodded in agreement.

However, my gut told me the Pringle guy wanted to connect with his birth family, not the authorities.

Biddy and I finished frosting the cookies before she had to meet Collin for dinner. During the entire visit, I'd been worried about slipping up and saying something about her surprise Paris trip. I rarely kept secrets from my best friend. This was the second one in the matter of two months.

Unable to put a hole through my best snowman cookie without it breaking, I glued a string to the back of the top and set it on the table to dry. That would make five ornaments on my tree.

After eating the last dish of ready-made mac and cheese, I threw on old jeans and a stained white T-shirt and started cleaning. I vacuumed up cobwebs from the master bedroom's ceiling, walls, and corners. Something I hadn't done in months. After cleaning the master bath, I reeked like bleach.

The doorbell rang.

Gretta marched inside with a determined look. "I wasn't there for my grandson the past thirty-one years. I need to be there for him now. Not only will I help him through this, but we'll prove he's not guilty."

"What if he *is* guilty? Are you prepared for that?"

"If he is guilty, then I'm to blame for having forced Maeve to put him up for adoption. He likely didn't have a proper upbringing. God only knows what he's been through."

"You can't blame yourself for the choices he's made."

"I have no plans to assist the authorities. Once we locate him, it'll be up to the lad to contact the detective. My gut tells me he's not guilty."

My gut *clenched* at the thought of learning the identity of a wanted criminal and not assisting the police. I had a nagging feeling there was more to the situation. That the Pringle guy maybe wasn't guilty. I couldn't get over the fact that a wanted criminal would take a DNA test and post it to the public. If his DNA had been found at a crime scene, there had to be a legit reason. Something seemed off.

What would I do if this was a close relation of mine? Before I'd identified Ian as my biological father, what if he'd taken a DNA test and the police were searching for him in connection to a crime? I'd see if we even located M.R. Pringle and then determine his crime. Yet should the severity of the crime justify me not telling the police and impeding *any* investigation? According to the law, if the police were using investigative genetic genealogy, it had to be a serious crime.

"Reactivate my accounts." Gretta pointed to my laptop on the cocktail table. "My cousin Millie is a nosey busybody. She has certainly had contact with the lad, wanting the skinny on him. I'll reach out to her."

A good thing I hadn't yet deactivated the accounts. I'd had an uneasy feeling Gretta was going to change her mind. I logged into her Ancestry.com account.

"I could contact her as your genealogist."

"No, I best do it if I have any chance of her replying."

What horrible thing had happened between Gretta and her cousin that they hadn't spoken for thirty years? My two sisters and I hadn't spoken in nearly a year because I'd inherited Grandma's house. In thirty years, if we still weren't speaking, would I regret not having a relationship with them? When and if I had regrets, I'd contact them. Biddy had been more of a sister to me than Emma or Mia.

"It's been over thirty years since you've spoken to her. You're going to need a great hook to get a response."

"She's a nosey goat. The fact that I had a visit from a detective will pique her interest. I won't say who or what it was about, just that I need to speak to her about it. That detective's visit was thanks to bad karma from that gingerbread castle. Had no choice but to offer our assistance to the baker."

"*Our* assistance?"

"He doesn't have enough helpers, so I told the store manager we'd assist. Otherwise, it won't be done in time for the New Year's auction."

"I can't even bake shortbread cookies." I could mix the ingredients. It was the rolling them out that was a nightmare.

"We'll merely be decorating the yoke."

"I can barely decorate cookies. Besides, my dad and Ian are going to be here."

"The more the merrier. Won't be needing to help out until a few days before New Year's. Would be nice if Rosie would assist since it was her nutmeg that caused the unfortunate accident."

As if Rosie had told Gretta to fight with the woman over a jar of stupid nutmeg. Rosie would have let the woman have the spice. I was in no frame of mind to argue with Gretta about not spending my holiday with Dad and Ian decorating gingerbread. The mere thought of the gingerbread castle induced a panic attack. I'd find volunteers to help out Gretta.

"I know he's not guilty." Gretta opened M.R. Pringle's profile. She gasped. "He was logged in today. He could be on right now. I know I promised Tommy I wouldn't contact him before talking to Maeve, but I feel like it's a sign." Gretta clicked on the messaging option and learned he wasn't accepting messages. "Do you think he has blocked just me, or everyone?"

"Your account was deactivated when he was on," I lied. *Had* he seen Gretta was a match? "So you're not the reason he turned it off." Fingers crossed. He'd possibly switched it off upon discovering his adoption, not wishing to be contacted.

"To think, mere hours ago my grandson was at his computer, viewing his account. At home, relaxing after he'd tucked his three children into bed." Gretta's eyes watered. "I might have great-grandchildren. Children who might need me should their father be sent..."

"Stay positive. Picture good thoughts."

It was much better than picturing her grandson behind bars.

## Five

THE MORNING FOG was lifting as I headed to the Ballycaffey cemetery to meet Edmond and decorate my grandparents' graves. I drove a narrow road to the abandoned medieval church and parked in front of a massive wrought iron gate with spear-tipped posts. I stepped from the car and snuggled into my green wool coat and red scarf. The wind whipped my hair against my face. I brushed away the hair and the tears warming my cool cheeks. A year ago I'd been here for Grandma's burial and had planned on selling her house. Now I was settled into the home and had a stable job rather than a new one every season.

I smiled, blinking the moisture from my eyes.

Grandma would be proud of me, especially my genealogy career.

A layer of pebbles or colored glass chippings covered the level ground in front of many of the newer graves toward the front. An Irish tradition, as were the evergreen wreaths, small mangers, and miniature Christmas trees decorating graves. Leaving the newer section behind, I traipsed through the tall grass covering a sloping hill, touching my foot cautiously on the uneven ground before placing my weight on it. I was afraid of tripping on a toppled-over tombstone, as Biddy had in the ghost hunters' video, or slipping into a sinkhole, like Biddy had done here when she was ten. Ivy-and-moss-covered tombstones and weathered Celtic crosses surrounded Grandma's and Grandpa's graves, located near her parents and grandparents. I'd recently cleaned the ivy from the older family stones to prevent the roots from causing them to split and crumble.

Edmond stood next to Grandma and Grandpa's granite tombstone. He wore the same pressed navy suit as he had last year when visiting the graves after Grandma's burial. However, he wasn't holding a glass of whiskey, and a nearly empty bottle wasn't sitting at his feet, by Grandma's glass of liquor.

Edmond smiled brightly, a sparkle in his blue eyes. "Lovely day to decorate the stones."

A bit of fog and drizzle. Perfect cemetery weather.

I slipped a mesh blanket of solar twinkle lights from my large purse and draped it over the tombstone.

"Was just telling Maggie about Rosie's Christmas present." He slipped a small velvet-covered box from his jacket pocket and opened it with shaky hands.

My eyes widened at the silver band with a pearl in the center and a diamond on each side.

He smiled nervously. "Think she'll fancy it, do you?"

"You're proposing to Rosie?"

He nodded. "Maggie approves, as did Emily. Just came from telling her."

"Of course they approve. Rosie is a wonderful person." I

gave Edmond a hug. "She's going to love it. It's perfect." Rosie was rarely seen without her pearl necklace on.

"She's quite a different woman than your grandmother." He smiled at the glass of whiskey he'd placed on the grave. "Would be putting a cuppa tea there for my Emily. And Maggie preferred a sturdy pair of wellies over fancy heels. Only recall having seen her in a dress on a few rare occasions. The same one, if I recall correctly. Blue with a few buttons on the front."

"Couldn't be exploring cemeteries in heels and a dress."

Edmond chuckled. "'Tis true." He massaged his stubbly chin. "Don't think I'm too old to be asking her hand in marriage?"

"A person is never too old to get married."

I was happy that Edmond was moving on. At the rate *I* was going, I might be Rosie's age when I got married.

When I returned from the cemetery, Biddy was waiting at the door, holding a platter of pastries. Delicate hollow cannoli-like ones, sugar-sprinkled rosettes—flower-shaped fried pastries—and other treats that contained my year's intake of butter or lard. We headed inside, and Biddy set the platter on the kitchen counter. She took off her green fleece jacket to reveal a green *Home Alone* sweatshirt that read *Merry Christmas, Ya Filthy Animal*. She was dressing quite festive this holiday season.

"The Norwegian woman up the road dropped off loads of these at the pub. They're lovely. Thought ya could be using some home-baked goods for your guests since we've eaten half the shortbread biscuits. And now that you're Norwegian, ya can get a taste for your heritage."

My most recent DNA test claimed I was 5 percent Norwegian. I had no known Scandinavian ancestors. Those sturdy genes were hanging on from the Viking warriors who'd invaded Ireland and Scotland. Ethnicities varied between DNA test sites. One company recently tweaked their estimates, and my Irish and English decreased by eight percent and Scottish appeared.

"Speaking of cookies, Gretta offered our assistance with decorating the gingerbread castle."

A horrified look seized Biddy's face. "Janey! Serious, are ya? As if I know how to be decorating a gingerbread castle. It took me a half hour to decorate that Christmas tree cookie, then I ate the bloody yoke. Unless this castle is for next year's toy drive, I don't see how we're going to be any help."

"I figure we can find volunteers."

Biddy snapped her fingers. "My auntie Violet used to work in a bakery. I'm sure she and Seamus would love to be helping out." Her gaze narrowed. "Except for Seamus's diabetes. Might be too much of a temptation for him. We'll just tell him it's not real gingerbread and candy."

The doorbell rang.

"If that's Gretta, don't mention the gingerbread castle," I said. "She's stressed out enough."

I answered the door, and Gretta stormed inside, fuming. "Heard back from that gobshite Cousin Millie." She snatched her phone from the outside pocket of her purse and read the message. "'Haven't seen ya in nearly thirty years and suddenly you're interested in the family and wanting to discuss a personal topic like DNA. I think not. Just being nosey, ya are. And I know exactly *who* you're wanting to discuss!'" Gretta's grip tightened around the phone. "Bet she knows the Pringle lad is my grandson. And the nosey goat likely knows even more than that. Surprised she didn't try to blackmail me to keep her gob shut. The woman has no scruples or money. I'm off to Galway. She will not get the best of me."

"Right now?" I said. "Can't we go after Christmas?"

She hadn't seen the woman in thirty years—another few days wouldn't matter as far as mending fences. And I really wanted to put off any further family DNA drama until after the holidays.

"My dad and Ian arrive in four days. I need to finish cleaning, grocery shop, and buy gifts. I can't go to Galway today."

Biddy's head snapped back in surprise. "Since when do materialistic gifts mean more than the gift of reuniting a grandmother with her grandson?"

When he was a wanted criminal.

"No worries," Gretta said. "I can be driving myself out to Galway. You needn't come along."

Rather than looking for pity, Gretta didn't appear to want us to tag along. Was her half-sibling story true and she didn't want that skeleton out of her closet? Regardless, she needed emotional support. Who knew what important info Millie might have on Gretta's grandson? And she couldn't be driving four to five hours round trip in her frazzled state. The last thing she needed was to get arrested for road rage. Biddy was right. Christmas wasn't about material gifts. Reuniting Gretta and her grandson was more important than golf balls.

"It's best we go along," I said. "I may need to analyze

your cousin's matches or question her if she made contact with your grandson."

"I can be taking snaps of any messages," Gretta said.

Biddy arched a curious brow. "Why don't ya want us going along?"

Gretta shrugged. "Didn't say that."

"Not to mention, you need someone who's calm and rational about the situation," I said. "I don't think either of you will be after seeing each other for the first time in thirty years."

"Suppose if you stay outside until we get things sorted and only come in should I need assistance with the genealogy, that would be fine. Millie likes strangers even less than she likes family."

I couldn't wait to meet Cousin Millie.

"Are ya sure this is the right road?" Biddy stared out the windshield at a herd of sheep trotting down the narrow lane. "Haven't seen a house for nearly two kilometers."

Which had taken twenty minutes to drive, thanks to the sheep. Set in the far west corner of Ireland, the Connemara was a mix of flat bogs and lakes giving way to rocky terrain and mountains. Its remote location was steeped in traditions, including Irish-speaking communities.

Hopefully, Cousin Millie spoke English.

"This is it," Gretta said in the backseat.

Biddy stopped at the end of a dirt drive leading to a weathered white cottage set near a cliff. The stone structure had battled the harsh winds and storms blowing in off the Atlantic Ocean for centuries. It had lost big time.

"Place looks deserted," Biddy said. "Sure this is it?"

White clouds of burning peat puffed up from the crumbling chimney into the air.

"She's here," Gretta said. "Can smell her."

My nose scrunched at an awful stench in the air—and it wasn't the earthy scent of burning peat.

Biddy drove cautiously up the drive, navigating around the potholes as best she could. Ivy crawled up the front of the house, covering all but one cracked window before disappearing under the metal roof. The window frame's peeling green paint matched the door. I couldn't imagine the house had electricity, let alone internet allowing us to view correspondence between M.R. Pringle and Cousin Millie.

Biddy and I happily remained in the car as Gretta had requested until she smoothed the way for me to be involved in a genealogy discussion. The cottage door opened, and instead of Millie slamming it in Gretta's face, Gretta stepped inside.

Biddy's top lip curled back. "What's that wretched smell?"

I smeared lavender-citrus-scented balm across my lips, then under my nose, inhaling a deep breath. The signature scent of Dalwade Castle's spa had helped me de-stress while searching for my uncle's killer. Thankfully, I'd bought two more tubes before leaving the hotel. Biddy doused the car in juniper sage spray. The calming spray about made me hack up a lung.

An ear-piercing squeal came from inside the house. We scrambled from the car as another squeal filled the air. I pounded on the wooden front door, driving a large splinter into my skin. I flinched in pain. The door swung open, and I forgot about my throbbing hand. There stood the muse for Edvard Munch's painting *The Scream*. The tall, thin woman with a freakishly long face had a ghostly complexion, sunken cheeks, and large gray eyes. A cigarette clung to a corner of her dry lips. A loosely tied sash hung around the waist of her filthy white robe, which covered the tops of army-green wellies. A squeal behind the woman startled Biddy and me.

Cousin Millie turned to a massive pig in a red-and-green knitted sweater lying in front of a roaring fire. "'Tis grand Birdie." Her gravelly two-pack-a-day voice cracked. "Merely more unwanted visitors."

Birdie. Cousin Millie's Ancestry.com profile name.

The woman waved us inside with her cigarette, ashes floating to the muddy, scarred wooden floor. "Born in a field, were ye? Be getting on inside before letting out the heat."

We stepped into the cold house, where wind howled through gaps between the window frames and the stone structure. The peat's woodsy scent struggled to camouflage the stench of cigarette smoke, dirty dishes filling the sink and counters, a pig, and a small dog curled up on a blue couch cushion sinking toward the floor. The pig snorted in disapproval at us, then went back to napping. Trophies and blue ribbons packed the fireplace mantel. Photos of Birdie boasting tiaras and satin sashes hung crooked on the cracked plaster wall.

"Still want to change your nickname?" I asked Biddy.

Her nose crinkled in disgust.

Nowhere to sit other than at the messy kitchen table next

to the scary woman and Gretta, who scowled at us for not staying in the car, we remained standing.

"So ya remember where I live, do ya?" Millie flicked her cigarette ashes on the table next to an overflowing ashtray. "Yet suppose ya couldn't forget." She smirked at Gretta. "Must be awfully desperate to learn who the fella is, having driven all this way to be apologizing to me."

Anger flashed in Gretta's gray eyes. "Drove all this way in the spirit of Christmas to provide *you* the opportunity to apologize to *me*."

I gave Gretta an encouraging nod, implying she should suck it up and apologize. Finding her grandson might rely on it.

"Sorry," Gretta snapped, shooting her gaze up at the rotting beams and remnants of straw thatching under the metal roof.

Millie's eyes widened in shock. "More desperate than I thought ya were. Why don't ya just message the Pringle fella if ya be needing to nose around in others' business?"

Gretta's jaw tightened.

"Or maybe he doesn't want to be talking with ya." Millie let out an annoyed grunt, sounding like Birdie. "He might have been upset learning he's me worthless dead brother's son. Fergus shagged half the women in Galway. Told him I hadn't a clue who his mother is."

"Crazy, are ya?" Gretta slammed a fist on the table, sending cigarette ashes flying. "The Pringle lad isn't Fergus's son."

"How much DNA do you share with him?" I asked.

The woman eyed a teacup collection on a wall shelf. She gestured to a dainty china cup with a picture of Birdie in a diamond tiara. "Be getting thirty euros for those at festivals. Suppose I could be parting with one for forty."

"Why would I be paying forty?" Gretta asked.

Her cousin shrugged, pushing back her wooden chair. "Best be tending to Birdie's rellies out back. Feeding time."

That was the stench in the air.

Gretta slipped two twenty-euro bills from her wallet. Millie snatched them from her hand and stuffed them inside one of her green wellies. She snubbed out her cigarette in the dainty teacup before setting it on the table in front of Gretta.

"Share about 200 cM with the fella," she said.

I stepped toward the table, shaking my head in disbelief. "You'd have to share around 1,700 average to be the guy's aunt."

"'Tis random the amount of DNA people share." Millie stuck her nose in the air, like a little miss know-it-all.

"It's not *that* random. Two hundred is the average shared by..." I wasn't about to confirm that at 200 shared cM, Pringle was Millie's first cousin twice removed and Gretta's grandson.

"People shouldn't be doing DNA testing if they aren't prepared to learn the truth," she said

"That's not the truth!" I wailed.

"If ya don't believe me, ya can be asking a genealogist."

"I *am* a genealogist. People shouldn't take DNA tests and give out incorrect information when they haven't a clue how to interpret the results. What if the guy gave up searching, thinking his father was dead?"

"Would appear he did. After I so generously gave him information on my eejit brother, only received a short thank-you. Need to be prepared for others to be discovering the skeletons in their closets, people do." She eyed Gretta, who shifted nervously in the creaky wooden chair.

Was Millie referring to Gretta's possible half sibling?

"How long ago were you in touch with him?" I asked.

She shrugged. "Six months or so."

Yet it didn't appear he'd given up his research, as he'd logged in yesterday and a week before that.

"Could we please see his messages?" I asked calmly.

The woman eyed a sheet of paper on the table. "Be needing to fill out the application for Birdie's entry in the plowing festival's livestock competition. Four-time winner, she is. Could win again if I wasn't a wee bit short on quid. Poor Birdie."

Birdie made a disgusting snort at the sound of her name.

Birdie's beauty queen days were long over.

"How much?" Gretta demanded.

"A hundred and twenty euros."

"For a pig's beauty contest?" Biddy said.

"She has over ten thousand followers on Facebook."

No way did Birdie have thousands of followers. My cemetery restoration page only had four hundred. Mostly thanks to that ghost hunters' video with Biddy stumbling over a fallen tombstone. Maybe I needed to increase the promo for the pets' burial section.

Gretta slipped two fifty euros from her wallet. "That's all I have."

Millie eyed Gretta's navy slacks and plain gray sweater. "Wearing those fancy clothes and that's all the quid ya got?"

The woman slid her gaze to Biddy and me.

"Mad, are ya?" Biddy said. "A hundred and twenty euros with nothing to show for it?"

"Take it or leave it," Millie snapped.

"Throw in another teacup," Biddy demanded.

I stared at Biddy in disbelief that she was bartering for souvenir pig teacups.

"Need the rest of them cups for the pageant, but guess I could be parting with a lighter." Millie pulled a red lighter from a stash in the kitchen drawer. She lit up a cigarette before handing over the lighter with a pic of Birdie that read *Smokin' Hot.*

Biddy and I each forked over ten euros.

Millie swept her cigarette toward Biddy. "Stand outside the living room window so I can be tossing ya the modem. Sketchy reception. Might even be having to go 'round back in there with the pigs so you can be facing west."

"I'll crawl up on the roof before I'll be getting in a pigpen." Biddy shot a wary glance up at the rotting beams supporting the metal roof as she headed outside.

Millie opened the window and tossed Biddy the small beat-up black box with faintly blinking lights. After trying several locations outside the pigpen, Biddy finally got the modem to provide intermittent internet access. M.R. Pringle's two messages to Millie were short. He referred to not having email access a few days while he and his mate went to view the Mirrie Dancers. My uncle Tavish had introduced me to the term common in northern Scotland and the Shetland Islands for the colorful shimmering northern lights that looked like dancers fluttering around the sky. Was the Pringle guy Scottish? He also mentioned being *scunnered*, which I believed was a Scottish term for tired. He signed off Andrew. Andrew Pringle? The *M.R.* weren't initials after all and likely stood for *mister*, just as we'd suspected. A mix of excitement and apprehension zipped through me.

We were one step closer to identifying Gretta's grandson.

Unless, of course, he was using a false name.

"Those messages are brilliant," Gretta said. "Could you be printing them off?"

Millie's hoarse laugh turned into a hacking cough.

My top lip curled back.

She cleared her throat. "Look like a Xerox machine, do I? Would fancy having a printer so I don't need to be driving three miles to the pub to use theirs."

"Can I take a picture of them?" I slipped my cell phone from my back pants pocket.

The woman slid a sideways glance over to a soiled blanket on the couch with pictures of Birdie on it.

"Eighty euros," Millie said.

I squared my shoulders. "Twenty."

"Seventy."

"Thirty."

"Sixty-nine." She held my gaze.

"Forty or no deal," I snapped. "Not like I can't remember what the messages say." But Gretta undoubtedly wanted a copy to reread the entire way home.

"Fifty and I'll throw in an ornament." She gestured to several plastic ornaments with Birdie in a Christmas sweater, hanging from a key rack by the door.

No way was I so desperate for ornaments that I'd be hanging one of a pig on my tree. But I was desperate for a copy of M.R. Pringle's messages. I forked over fifty euros, and Millie tossed the smelly blanket and ornament onto a kitchen chair. I snapped photos of the messages. Biddy tossed the modem through the window and onto the couch. I grabbed the pig souvenirs and bolted out the front door, Gretta hot on my heels.

Biddy joined us en route to the car as Millie shouted out, "How's it feel being back *home*? Miss the house, don't ya?"

Gretta had once lived in that dump?

Another squeal filled the air before the door slammed shut.

"At least Birdie has Christmas gifts for Collin now," I said jokingly, ignoring Millie's rude comment.

*"Birdie?"* Biddy smacked me on the arm.

"Sorry. I meant Biddy."

She gave me a skeptical look. "Can be putting them in one of the gift hampers at the next tractor run. Except, of course, the ornament would be lovely hanging on your tree next to Abraham Lincoln." Biddy stuck the stinky items in the trunk and doused them with juniper spray, along with us, before she allowed anyone in her car.

Gretta shook her head in defeat. "Guess my grandson *could* be a criminal. After all, he shares DNA with that wretched woman."

We sat in silence as Biddy drove down the narrow road, the dilapidated dwelling disappearing in the distance. The windows were open, the heat cranked, trying to get rid of the stench from Millie's house. I finally managed to squeeze the large sliver from my hand and flicked it out the window. Nurse Biddy had a first-aid kit in the glove compartment.

After using an antiseptic wipe to clean away the dried blood, I stuck a Band-Aid on the wound.

"Take the next left," Gretta blurted from the backseat.

"We came in on this road," Biddy said

"Left!" Gretta demanded as we came upon an unmarked road.

Biddy took a sharp turn onto a lane with a strip of tall grass and weeds growing up the center. She slammed on the brakes and shot an angry look over her shoulder at Gretta. "Janey! Ya nearly gave me a heart attack. This is a shortcut for cows, not cars. I won't be driving down this road."

"It's the only way to get there." Gretta peered out the window, a faraway look in her eyes. "Please keep driving."

I nodded for Biddy to continue on.

Thankfully, we didn't encounter a herd of sheep until we came upon them grazing among weathered Celtic crosses and tombstones rising up from the overgrown, uneven terrain. A crumbling stone wall provided a partial view of the Atlantic and a landscape of mountains in the distance.

"This is it," Gretta muttered.

Biddy pulled into a faint outline of a path buried beneath weeds, leading through an ivy-wrapped rusted gate hanging by one hinge. We once again sat in silence. Usually I was the first one to race into a cemetery and the last one out. Gretta needed to take the lead on this one. After a few minutes, she stepped from the car.

"What if she means this is *it, it*?" Biddy said. "Like she's going to hurl herself off the cliff?"

Waves rolled in from the Atlantic and crashed against the shore below a low-lying cliff. "We should go with her. Stay behind and give her space. If she heads toward the water, we'll run over and tackle her."

We closed the windows, then stepped from the car. Several large sheep moseyed over near the entrance, eying us with curiosity. Biddy stared down a large one with a splash of blue dye across its wool. He blinked first and went back to eating.

"Do you have Froot Loops in your purse?" Biddy asked.

"As if I carry a baggie of cereal in my purse to appease a whiny toddler. When have I ever taken Pinky on a road trip?"

This would be the third cemetery Biddy had been in since she was ten and her foot slipped into a grave's sinkhole. The first one, last Christmas, someone had locked us in. Since it had likely been Gretta, I didn't see that happening again. However, I couldn't promise that we wouldn't come across a dead body on a grave rather than *in* it, like when I'd discovered one on my grandparents' graves. A *living* soul undoubtedly hadn't been in the abandoned graveyard for decades.

Standing at the entrance, Gretta peered out at the desolate landscape. A breeze blew off the ocean, whipping my hair across my face and sending a chill through me. Gretta headed past the rusty gate and into the graveyard. Biddy and I trailed behind, stepping cautiously on the ground. Gretta paused in front of a few tombstones too weathered to read and continued on. Too bad I hadn't driven. I kept a stash of tinfoil in my car trunk to help decipher stones.

Gretta paused, then knelt in front of a grave. She began frantically uprooting handfuls of long grass and whipping the clumps to the side. We took a few tentative steps toward her, wanting to respect her privacy. Her body trembled, and she wrapped herself in a hug. We joined Gretta, each placing a comforting hand on a shoulder.

Several thorny branches scratched against a lichen-and-moss-covered tombstone. The stone's worn engraving read Cormac and Gretta Mulkerrin, Gretta's maternal grandparents. Gretta placed a hand against the small stone for her mother Annie Mulkerrin, who'd died nearly sixty years ago. My eyes watered at the neglected stones.

"This is the first I've visited my mother's grave." Gretta let out a shaky breath. "I was a horrible daughter."

"A lot of people don't handle death well," I said.

Biddy nodded. "Everyone deals with grief differently."

"Not sure if I grieved or not," Gretta muttered. "Makes me an even worse daughter. I was raised by an unwed teenage mother. I never knew my father."

Gretta's story about a half sibling could be true. However, the name and death date she'd provided for her father were apparently false.

Gretta brushed her trembling fingers over the dates engraved on her grandmother's tombstone. "The death dates I gave you for both my grandparents were wrong. And I had my grandmother's first name as Anna. I forgot I was named after her." She cupped a hand over her mouth and choked back tears. "Please be sure to change those in my tree."

I snapped a photo of the graves. "I'll update it."

"I must replace this stone with a proper one. She was a good person. Worked hard to provide for me. I didn't appreciate her strength. I wanted to be put up for adoption, hoping we could both have better lives. Who does that? Asks their mother to give them away to strangers. Like I forced my daughter to do. I'd felt if I'd had a difficult life despite a loving mother who'd wanted me, what kind of a life could Maeve have given her child?"

"Does Maeve know about this?" I asked.

Gretta shook her head. "Only Tommy."

"Maybe you should tell her. Might make her more sympathetic and understanding about why you'd insisted on the adoption. And that you're now trying to make amends and face your past by finding your grandson."

Using a ragged fingernail, Gretta managed to peel a clump of moss from the headstone. "I should have this properly cleaned."

I stopped myself from offering to see about having the cemetery cared for. One restoration project at a time.

However, I could add a bit of holiday cheer. I went to the car and returned with my purse. I slipped out an extra string of twinkle lights I hadn't needed for my grandparents' tombstone and wrapped it securely around her mother's stone. Rifling through the bottom of my purse, I found a half dozen red and green foil-covered chocolates from McCarthy's pub. I handed them to Gretta, who placed the festive candies by the grave.

Gretta managed a faint smile. "She loved chocolate. And animals. She was always taking in strays..."

She reminisced about her mother until it started to rain a half hour later. She left the cemetery more at peace than when we'd arrived. Thankfully, I'd taken the time to come with her. Reuniting family, except for Cousin Millie, was much more important than cleaning, buying gifts...or anything else.

## Six

THE RIDE HOME from County Galway seemed twice as long as the ride there. Gretta sat in silence, reflecting on her cemetery visit. I'd worn off a pound or two shivering from our windows cracked to air out the vehicle. Biddy and I tossed around ideas for Collin's gift. I wanted to tell her that materialistic gifts weren't important, like she'd told me when I'd complained about going to Galway. Since Collin was taking her to Paris, she'd kill me if she'd only gotten him a box of candy. Dozens of ideas later, cookie ornaments were still at the top of her list.

An impressive wrought iron gate opened to a paved drive leading back to the Lynch's two-story stone house with a yellow door and window trim. Colorful twinkle lights blanketed the shrubs in front. The door swung open, sending the green decorative wreath flying from its nail to the ground. Tommy stomped out onto the stoop, fists on his hips. Gretta let out a distressed groan, dragging herself from the backseat.

She told Tommy about our visit with Cousin Millie.

Concern filled his eyes. He placed a hand gently on Gretta's shoulder. "Dying, are ya?"

"No, I'm perfectly healthy. Just needed to see what she might be knowing about our grandson."

Relief washed over the man, and he wrapped Gretta in a tight embrace. "We'll figure this whole thing out. It'll be grand. And I agree—you should be telling Maeve your past was at least partly why you'd insisted on the adoption. And you're right. Ya shouldn't have been handling Maeve's pregnancy on your own."

Biddy and I were still crying from the sentimental scene when we arrived at McCarthy's pub. I decided to walk home and wear off a few bites of all the cookies I'd been eating. She headed inside the pub, and a few seconds later, Collin bolted out, waving for me to wait.

"Biddy went to change." He sniffed the air around me. "Were you two out farming today?"

"It's a long story. I'm sure she'll tell you."

"Have you thought of any sites Biddy might be wanting to see?"

"You guys are only going to have a few days. I would hit the highlights, like the Eiffel Tower."

"Already booked that one. I want the trip to be perfect."

Wow, he was nervous about making the trip perfect...

"Are you going to propose at the top of the Eiffel Tower?" I snapped my mouth shut, unable to believe I'd just blurted out the question.

The color drained from Collin's face. "Why would you be thinking that?"

"Sorry. I just know somebody else who's getting engaged

at Christmas so I have proposals on the brain. And Paris is such a romantic setting."

"Is *Biddy* going to think I'm proposing if I take her to Paris?" His breathing quickened, and he raked a nervous hand through his hair.

"No, I'm sure she won't."

"*You* just thought it. Jaysus, I can't be taking her there if she's going to be expecting me to propose."

"She won't."

Collin's panicked gaze darted around. "I need to cancel the trip. Doubt I'll be able to book a hotel in Dublin this close to New Year's Eve."

My heart raced. "You can't cancel the trip. You'll never get a room in Dublin. Your plane tickets are likely nonrefundable. Your friend's sister will be upset she has nobody to watch her place or her cat." Most importantly, if Biddy ever learned she'd missed out on a trip to Paris because of *me*, she'd kill me! "Just cancel the Eiffel Tower ticket. Take her somewhere less romantic."

"Where in Paris isn't romantic?" He tossed his arms up in frustration.

"Tell her about the trip at Christmas. If you're not sweeping her off to Paris last minute, she won't be thinking you might plan to propose."

Collin shook his head and bolted back toward the pub.

"Don't cancel!" I yelled after him.

I was desperate for Biddy to spend New Year's Eve in Paris while I spent it alone at home undoubtedly eating store-made lasagna. If it weren't for the fact that Detective Brennan was trying to arrest Gretta's grandson and I'd been a bit confrontational, I'd consider asking him out for New Year's.

Upon arriving home, I stripped off my stinky clothes, showered with lavender bath gel, and slipped into my flannel jammies. Sitting on the living room couch with my laptop and a cup of tea, I checked out Birdie's Facebook fan page. The pig didn't have ten thousand fans. She had nearly *eleven* thousand! Seriously? I scanned hundreds of photos, including one of Birdie dressed up for Halloween in a blond wig, shimmering silver dress, and sash that read *Miss Piggy*. Millie was dressed as Kermit in a green knitted frog hat, green clothes, and green-painted skin. The photo was the banner for a costume-party event at a pub where they'd won second place. Birdie and Millie had dozens of events listed. I wasn't about to tell Gretta how impressed I was with Birdie's page and that I envied her nasty cousin's marketing skills.

While on Facebook, I went to my community action reward post. Some guy offered to buy the golf balls for a discounted rate because they were personalized. I didn't *have* the golf balls. It was an action group, not a marketplace.

I perused people-search sites for an Andrew Pringle in Scotland. Not a lot of Pringles and none with the first name Andrew. However, people could usually request to have themselves removed from those sites. Hundreds of Andrews, Andy, and Drew Pringles came up on social media world-wide. I checked for an M.R. Pringle, in case they were his initials and Andrew was a nickname or a fake name for privacy purposes. Not one.

I decided to run Andrew's slang terms past Ian. According to online sources, scunnered was a Scottish term, as was Mirrie Dancers. A valid reason to call Ian, even though I'd be seeing him in a few days. I needed to casually fish for gift ideas.

"You'd hear scunnered mainly in Glasgow," Ian said. "It's known as Glaswegian slang. Why? Did someone say he was scunnered and you hadn't a clue what he meant?"

I explained my research for Gretta without disclosing her name, since the two would likely meet during his visit. I also mentioned the visit from Detective Brennan.

"That's a bit worrisome, isn't it?" he said.

"Hopefully, it doesn't turn out to be anything too bad. Yet law enforcement isn't allowed, legally anyway, to load DNA on the site unless it's a major crime."

"Been watching a show on solving cold cases using genetic genealogy. That's pure dead brilliant. The UK should permit authorities to use it. Amazing how a genealogist can find matches who share second great-grandparents. You'd do a fab job at it."

"Way more people are interested in doing it than there are jobs. Besides, I have more than I can handle between paid work and the mystery cases I've been solving the past year. Like this woman's DNA case."

"The world is merely on the cusp of this method for criminal investigation. A few years and loads of third-party companies offering the service will be popping up. That means there'll be more shows on the telly. Binged-watched that one in two days. Missing Rhona something fierce, and she just flew out three days ago."

Rhona was the love of his life and the widowed wife of

his murdered brother Malcolm. She was visiting her daughter, who went to college in Melbourne. I hoped one day soon I'd get to meet my only first cousin.

I recommended a few other genealogy-related shows to Ian. It was cool that his interest in my profession had him binge-watching shows that we could sit and talk about.

I filled him in on my bizarre road trip to Cousin Millie's. "That pig has nearly eleven thousand Facebook fans. Should have had Ava and you decorate the pet cemetery. Granted, Birdie is alive and offers great photo ops dressing up in holiday sweaters and crowns. Still, I could decorate Princess Beatrice's tombstone with a crown and royal robe. Something to attract more cat fans. The pet cemetery shows at least some of the Kerr family had a sense of humor and love for animals."

*Princess Beatrice. Born a cat, lived like a lion.*

"What about instead of Christmas you celebrate birthdays?" Ian said. "Most stones have the animals' death years and ages. Could highlight one each day in January. I have a meeting there in two weeks. Could decorate the graves with birthday hats and streamers to take snaps."

"Excellent idea. If there's a fan base for a pig, there must be one for Enid the cow, who produced sixteen calves and loads of milk. Several of the animals died in the 1900s. I bet some historical family photos include the pets they obviously adored. Photos would be great promo. I'll contact Archie about that." The castle's owner was up for anything that brought in business. The man had dressed up like a milking maid. Maybe I'd plan a trip there during Ian's meeting and then decorate the graves with him. I could spend time looking through old photos. One of my favorite pastimes.

Brainstorming the cemetery project with Ian and his belief that Andrew Pringle was from Glasgow had put a bounce in my step. Yet I still had no gift ideas unless I could find one of those genealogy shows on DVD. Did they even sell DVDs anymore?

I went back to searching for M.R. Pringle. People often used the same profile name for every site. I came across a few posts on genealogy forums six months ago by M.R. Pringle. In one he mentioned a possible paternal connection to the surname Bodkin. He signed off *A. Bodkin(?)*.

Another clue that his name was likely Andrew.

I checked the online white pages and other sites for the unfamiliar surname Bodkin in the Ballycaffey area. None came up. The family may have moved away over the past thirty-one years, especially if a man's wife had discovered his affair with Maeve. Or maybe Andrew was clueless about DNA research and how to determine accurate connections, same as Cousin Millie. His Bodkin theory might have been based on a few distant relations with the surname.

GenDNA allowed me to view the matches that Gretta *didn't* share in common with Andrew. No Bodkin matches. A lot of matches used cryptic profile names. Also, Bodkin could be a female ancestor's maiden name in a family line. Or had Andrew taken a Y-DNA test enabling him to trace his male lineage and the surname had shown up? With a Y-DNA test, you were lucky if even fifty percent of your matches shared the same surname. I knew people who didn't even have *one* match with their surname. Through the centuries, surnames often changed due to adoptions, children born out of wedlock, and numerous other reasons.

I reviewed Ireland's 1854 Griffith's Valuation. Most

Bodkins had lived in the Galway area. The 1911 census listed fewer Bodkin families, but still mostly Galway. Gretta was married in Salthill, west of Galway city. She'd once mentioned her sons Ian and Rory went to the university there. Maeve might have been visiting her brothers and hooked up with one of their friends or some random guy at a party. It would be wonderful if the baby's father wasn't a local.

However, if he was a local, someone at the pub would surely have known any Bodkins who'd lived in the area in the past thirty-one years. The locals knew everything that went on in the community and forgot nothing. I changed out of my jammies and into clean clothes, then headed to the pub.

I entered McCarthy's, filled with lively chatter rather than Christmas music or patrons cheering for their favorite dart player on TV. Finally. A reprieve from the boring *sport*. Thankfully, Collin had left, and Biddy had a pepperoni pizza hot out of the oven sitting on the bar. I slid onto a corner stool and joined her, telling her about my Bodkin find.

"Never heard of the name." Biddy peered over at her mom pouring me a cider. "Ever known any Bodkins in the area?"

Ita shook her head. "Don't recall having known a Bodkin *anywhere*. Why you looking for one?"

"Genealogy research," I said.

Ita nodded in understanding. Biddy and I often confided in her mom about our mystery cases when we sometimes shouldn't. We couldn't betray Gretta's trust.

Biddy stared at the pizza while I scarfed down a piece. "Aren't you hungry?"

She shook her head. "Collin made up some lame excuse about not being able to stay for dinner. Something's up. He's acting strange."

I choked on my cider, then cleared my throat. "Why?"

"I get the feeling he's wanting to back out on our New Year's Eve in Dublin." She plucked a pepperoni from the pizza. "What if he's going to break up with me? How depressing if I get dumped on the holidays."

My heart raced. "You aren't going to get dumped. Collin is mad about you."

And he was taking Biddy to Paris whether he wanted to or not! I polished off four pieces of pizza while Biddy ate the pepperoni off two slices. I gave her a pep talk about how Collin was crazy for her and they'd have a great time in Dublin. We circulated the pub, hoping to find someone familiar with the surname Bodkin. We went to our two stocky friends, John Deere and Beckham.

"Ever heard of any Bodkins in the area?" I asked.

Johnny's gaze narrowed. "Think the fella who nicked your package was named Bodkin, do ya?"

How would I know the thief's last name? He apparently followed the community action page.

"No, this is about something else."

"Mickey Doolin's wife had a package nicked right out of her hand walking out of a Dublin mall two days ago," Beckham said.

"People go mad 'round the holidays." Johnny shook his head, then peered over at me with a smile. "Met your new fella. Seems like a nice lad. A brilliant hurler."

I gave him a baffled look.

"The fella in the suit. Was pulling out your drive when I was walking Misty. Stopped to ask me if he was heading in the right direction for Navan. Had a sticker on his car for the hurling championship two years back. Quite the match, it was."

"He's not a professional hurler or my boyfriend."

John Deere was making local gossip Marjorie the Mouth look like a rookie lately.

He chuckled. "Ah, no, not a professional hurler. Played for Navan's GAA. My nephew was on the losing team. Poor lad. At least he'd made it that far before heading off to university."

Biddy's nose wrinkled in confusion. "That Brennan fella isn't old enough to have had a kid playing for the GAA."

Johnny gave his head a frustrated shake. "No, the lad himself was in the tournament. Said he scored the winning point." The man scooped up a handful of foiled chocolates from the bowl on the bar, and he and Beckham went back to playing darts.

"Even if he received his leaving cert two years ago, how could Detective Brennan have finished training and gained enough experience to be a detective in some special unit?" Biddy said.

Hmm... Something was fishy.

We sat at a corner table and researched the training and experience needed for Ireland's law enforcement careers. The NSU required two years garda training and three years of service before being considered for a specialist unit, which undoubtedly required training itself.

"No way could that *detective* have already reached that rank," Biddy said.

I'd been debating asking out the sketchy guy, who was barely of age!

"Maybe John Deere is confused about the hurling match," I said. "Maybe it took place *ten* years ago, not *two*."

"That must be it. We couldn't have been duped by the fella. Could we?"

Certainly wouldn't be the first time we'd been duped.

John Deere's previous leads had helped in solving several mysteries. Even though his stories often sounded embellished, they'd proven true and spot-on.

If this one was spot-*on*, something was *off*.

I pulled up a social media page for the hurling club near Navan. After scrolling back through two years of photos, I came upon one of the famous championship. *Detective Brennan* stood in the back row center, holding up the team's trophy, peering at me with those dreamy blue eyes. Players' names weren't listed.

Biddy dropped back against the chair. "We were duped."

At least I hadn't been double-duped and asked the guy out for New Year's Eve.

## Seven

THE MOST LIKELY place to find someone able to identify our bogus Detective Brennan was the Navan mall. Seeing as he'd asked John Deere for directions to Navan, that was where he possibly still lived. The following morning, we arrived at the mall five minutes after stores opened. The last place I wanted to be six days before Christmas. Filled with panicked shoppers, mostly men wanting opinions on women's gifts, it was crazier than the grocery store. Wanting to escape the madhouse as quickly as possible, Biddy and I made a beeline for two older teenage girls admiring holiday party dresses in a store window. I showed the girls the hurling championship photo on my phone.

The blond girl with long fake eyelashes dressed in jeans and a pink sweater wore a dreamy smile. "That'd be Noah Kenny. Fierce gorgeous, isn't he? Was at the hurling match when he scored the winning point."

"Do you know if he's still in the area?" I asked.

"Down in Templemore, Tipperary, training to be a guard."

The dark-haired girl in a green sweater with glittery silver eyeshadow shook her head. "Was kicked out of the schooling. Haven't a clue why. Saw him over in Trumone working at a petrol station. The one with the lovely lattes."

"Is he, now?" An intrigued smile curled the blond girl's hot-pink lips.

Biddy and I thanked the girls, then took off before they questioned our interest in Noah, wondering if we were ga-ga over the guy like every other girl. As if we could compete with those two fashion divas. Biddy in her Griswold Family Christmas sweatshirt and me in a boring blue sweater. Neither of us with makeup on, our hair in ponytails. Besides, I certainly wasn't ga-ga over Noah. Once again why I couldn't let looks influence my attraction to a man.

We headed toward the parking ramp, off to the petrol station before the blond girl went there for a chai latte and to flutter her fake lashes at Noah. If she blabbed about our encounter, she'd ruin our element of surprise.

"Can't believe we were scammed by a garda flunky." Biddy fumed as she hopped into her car. "Actually, she didn't even say he'd flunked out. He'd been *kicked* out. How do ya get kicked out of garda training?"

"Better question, *why* were we scammed? He obviously isn't legit or involved with a cold case, so why'd he make up that story?"

"Playing a prank, was he?"

"He can't see Gretta's DNA matches without being a match himself or a match's match on GenDNA. Unless he *is* somehow associated with law enforcement."

"I guess we'll have to be asking Noah Kenny ourselves."

Ten minutes later, we pulled into Trumone's parking lot

and parked next to a black car with a hurling championship sticker on the back passenger window. A hurling stick, discarded takeaway bags, and a wrinkled black suit were on the backseat.

"Probably his parents' car," Biddy said.

We marched inside, where Noah stood behind a cash register dressed in a green store-logoed polo shirt and tan slacks. I convinced myself he wasn't nearly as attractive without the black suit and purple tie. He spotted us, and his gaze darted to his coworker ringing up a customer. He placed a hushing finger to his lips as we approached.

"I'm undercover," he whispered. "What can I be helping you ladies with?" He flashed me a sly smile, and my jaw tightened.

And here I'd been so proud of myself for firing questions at this yahoo and making him nervous.

"Looking for *Detective* Noah Kenny," Biddy said.

The guy cussed and darted around the counter and out a side door to the parking lot. We raced after him in case he was attempting to flee.

He came to an abrupt halt and spun around toward us. "Who told you my name?"

"We can't *divulge* our sources," Biddy said, throwing his favorite go-to word back at him.

He raked a frustrated hand through his dark hair. "I was going for Colin Farrell. Thought I'd nailed the part."

"We knew something was fishy right from the start," I lied. "You might have gotten away with it if you hadn't stopped my neighbor to ask for directions."

He smacked a palm against his forehead and groaned. "A rookie mistake. Please don't be telling the fella who hired me, or I won't get the other three hundred euros and a chance at getting back into garda training."

Biddy's jaw dropped. "A fella paid ya six hundred euros to scam us?"

"We won't say a word if you can answer a few questions," I said. How could we tell his employer unless he gave us the name?

He nodded.

"Who hired you?" I demanded.

"Haven't a clue. Got an email from the fella. Said I'd come highly recommended."

"Highly recommended?" Biddy scoffed. "You were kicked out of garda training. He hired ya because you're gullible and desperate."

His shoulders snapped back, thrusting out his chest. "In all fairness to me, it wasn't my fault. This is a chance for me to rebuild my reputation and become a national hero."

"Why hire *you* and not a professional?" I said.

"The fella said he was walking a fine line with Ireland's privacy law. I figured I'd be doing the country a massive service putting the bloke in prison."

"So the supposed crime occurred in Ireland and not the US, if you'd be a hero *here*," I said.

He nodded faintly. "Suppose so."

"If you don't have a name, what makes you think it's a fella?" Biddy asked.

"From the email address."

Biddy gazed expectantly at him. "Which is?"

"I can't be divulging confidential information in a case that could lead to the conviction of a wanted felon. Besides, he wrote me a script on what to be saying, and his wording sounded like a man."

Biddy rolled her eyes. "Man or woman, the person who hired ya might not be in law enforcement. If he is, he isn't legit. Or it could be some stalker chick trying to hunt the fella down. If she kills him, it's on you."

The guy's eyes widened with panic.

I shot Biddy a cautious glance to cut back on the drama. "A crazy ex would know the guy's identity and hire a private detective or hitman to hunt him down. She wouldn't go the DNA route. This mystery man who hired you might be in Ireland, not the US."

"He's in Scotland. At least the IP address for his email is some place in Scotland."

Biddy and I exchanged intrigued glances.

Scotland? Where M.R. Pringle likely lived?

Biddy looked mildly impressed. "Fair play to ya, checking on the IP address."

Noah smiled proudly.

"Do you recall where in Scotland?" I asked.

"Hollyshock or something like that."

I searched the town online. "Holyhock?"

He snapped his fingers. "That's it."

I looked it up on a map. "It's an hour south of Edinburgh. Near Roxburghshire, where the Pringle surname originated hundreds of years ago. Likely a coincidence."

Yet was it merely a coincidence that this mystery man was located within a hundred miles of Glasgow, where our Pringle guy possibly lived?

"Do you know where in Holyhock?" Biddy asked.

He shook his head. "An IP address won't pin the exact location."

At least I hadn't been attracted to a complete idiot.

"If M.R. Pringle is also in Scotland, that means the mystery man might be closing in on him," I told Biddy.

"Fella also could have rerouted his IP address so it'd look like he's in Scotland when he's not," Noah said.

"Is that easy to do?" I asked.

He nodded. "But doubt most people know it's easy and wouldn't think of doing it."

Biddy and I wouldn't have had a clue.

"Yet if the fella is trying to throw someone off his track, why not reroute it to a city where it's harder to find a person?" he said.

"Show us the emails," I said.

"I can't be doing that. National security is at stake."

"We'll turn you in for impersonating a detective," Biddy said. "You'll never get back into garda training."

"You can't prove I did that."

I slipped his business card from my purse.

"Haven't a clue what that is."

"Easy enough for us to get your fingerprints off it," Biddy lied. Her gaze darted to me. "That garda fella owes us a favor."

Garda Higgins owed us big time. When Biddy and I'd uncovered the skeleton, her car was held at the scene until it could be searched for skeletal remains or other evidence lodged in the vehicle's undercarriage. Her car disappeared, supposedly removed by the forensics team for further investigation. We later learned Garda Higgins was driving it for personal use. He'd hit hard times, and Biddy had taken pity on him rather than getting him fired and making his life even worse. Thanks to Biddy's sympathetic attitude, the officer owed us a favor.

I nodded. "Yep. Guess we'll be calling in that favor. And my neighbor who gave you directions saw you pulling out of my driveway. Helping us might also make you a hero if we uncover a dirty cop or an illegit operation going on."

Noah's shoulders dropped in defeat. "Suppose I can be reading them to ya."

His annoyed coworker stuck his head out the door. "Think you're on bloody holiday, do ya?"

"My granny was just taken to the A and E, ya eejit."

The guy's jaw dropped. "Ah, sorry 'bout that. Hope she's grand." He ducked back inside.

"The grieving grandson?" Biddy said. "Another role ya nailed?"

Noah smirked, pulling up the emails on his phone. The mystery man's initial message said he needed someone to visit Gretta to discuss her DNA relation and request her assistance in cracking a five-year-old cold case. He provided directions to her house and the script for Noah to follow. The person hadn't responded to Noah's email informing him that Gretta's match was a half sibling.

"I used my genealogy email address for Gretta's GenDNA account. That could have narrowed her location down to County Westmeath. If this person *isn't* a cop, why is he looking for M.R. Pringle?" I mused. "And how does he have access to Gretta's matches? A person has to spit in a tube to have DNA analyzed and uploaded to test sites. Fingernails, toothbrush, none of that can be tested as of yet.

Only law enforcement can load DNA from items found at crime scenes."

"Maybe it was a legit officer who uploaded the DNA but a crooked garda is after that Pringle fella," Noah said.

Inspiration lit Biddy's face. "Maybe he's in the witness protection program and it's the bad guys trying to identify him. Or he witnessed a crime and is on the run because he knows a crooked cop is after him."

"We need to figure out the identity of this mystery man." I tapped a finger against my lips. "Let's plan a sting operation."

Noah looked baffled.

No wonder this kid was kicked out of garda training.

"A sting operation is used to catch someone attempting to commit a crime. An undercover officer pretends to be a criminal's partner or the possible victim and plays along with a suspect's plan while gathering evidence of the crime."

The guy nodded eagerly. "I can be doing that. You have to admit I had you two going until your neighbor blew my cover."

Sad, but true.

"We'll have you send an email claiming that Gretta Lynch contacted you with important info on her supposed half-sibling DNA match. However, it was complicated and best discussed over the phone, so there was no paper trail. And we need to determine if this guy is in Scotland."

"Best be writing this down," Noah said.

"I'll text you a brief script."

"With all these scripts, maybe I should be becoming an actor rather than a garda." He flashed me a sexy grin and strolled inside the petrol station.

I rolled my eyes. Yet I hated to admit he'd nailed the role of Detective Brennan.

"Who'd have hired that eejit?" Biddy said. "Why would a law enforcement officer not have hired a skilled detective for such an important case?"

"Because he's skirting Ireland's privacy law and has to pay for help out of his own pocket when illegally investigating using DNA. Maybe a teacher from his garda school knows Noah would jump at the chance to redeem himself. If it's not a cop who created the GenDNA account, the only people who would have access to M.R. Pringle's Ancestry.com account would be the man himself or a genealogist managing his account. A genealogist wouldn't have blocked his account's messenger service. The person would have messaged Gretta. And would have an adoptee's DNA loaded to every possible site, not merely two, not knowing where he might connect with a relation who was close enough to provide clues. And sites outside of Ancestry.com have more advanced chromosome browsers for serious DNA analysis."

"The lengths this person is going to in finding this Pringle fella makes it seem more dangerous than the authorities looking for a criminal in a cold case. It's too weird. And scary if this mystery fella is in Scotland and closing in on Gretta's grandson."

Biddy was right. Things were heating up. Just how far would this person go to find Andrew, and what would he do when he did?

We needed to locate Gretta's grandson first.

Hopefully, the mystery man responded to Noah's email.

☘ ☘

Biddy drove while I texted Noah his four-line script to send our mystery man. I ordered him not to deviate from it. I called and asked Gretta to meet at my house. Despite Tommy becoming more understanding about her quest to find their grandson, I preferred to keep my distance from him until it was all worked out. He knew about my involvement with Gretta's DNA test. Hopefully he didn't blame me.

Biddy pulled into my driveway, and Gretta sprang from the front porch stoop and onto her feet. We went into the living room, where I recounted our visit with Noah Kenny.

"The lad should be put in jail, he should." Gretta's long, thin fingers balled into fists. She'd knock the guy flat if he were here. "Pretending to be a detective, making me think my grandson's a criminal." The angry look on her face faded. "At least now we know he's not a wanted man."

"He's still *wanted* for some reason," I said. "If not by the authorities, then by who, and why?"

"Perhaps Mr. Pringle is an undercover detective," Biddy mused. "While working a case, his cover was blown, so he had to go into hiding. Could be a crooked cop nicked a few strands of hair from Pringle's brush and uploaded his DNA to secretly help the bad guys find him. Maybe Pringle was part of a sting operation, like you were talking about earlier."

Gretta nodded enthusiastically. "That's brilliant. I knew he was a good man, not a criminal."

My head spinning, I held up a halting hand. "That scenario makes no sense. The crooked cop would have to already know Pringle's identity. The DNA wouldn't help the bad guys find him."

"It could have if Gretta had known her grandson's location and told Noah," Biddy said.

True...

"We still need to keep an open mind despite all these possible theories."

Gretta's eyes widened. "Bet my wretched Cousin Millie is behind it all. After our visit she posted our genealogy scenario with Mr. Pringle to some online group. The members informed her the lad is my grandson. Got a message from her an hour ago demanding money to keep her gob shut about my family secret. Wants me to pay up before New Year's. I even said before we went to see the nasty woman that she was capable of blackmail."

Biddy gasped. "Maybe she knew your relation to him *before* we visited and lied saying she thought she was his aunt. *She* hired Noah to play detective and make you believe your grandson was a wanted criminal so she could blackmail you. And now she's pretending like she just figured it all out."

Gretta nodded. "Getting me over to her house so she could scam money from me wasn't enough."

"She's not on GenDNA," I said. "She couldn't have known you're on there unless she deleted her account after she saw your profile and before I saw hers." I shook my head. "I don't think Millie's bright enough to put together this scheme, especially not rerouting an IP address. The woman has to throw her modem out the window to get internet service."

"Maybe she doesn't," Biddy said. "Maybe that was all for show, when actually she's a tech guru."

I rolled my eyes.

"Okay, maybe not a guru, but smart enough to hire someone."

Her Facebook page *was* quite impressive.

"That would mean Pringle manages the Casper account, not some cop or bad guy," I said.

"If Millie seriously thought Mr. Pringle was her brother Fergus's son, he might have an inheritance due," Gretta said. "Fergus made a decent living as an engineer. At least last I knew. Maybe he left his money to an heir, and when one couldn't be located, it went to Millie." She gazed at the flames dancing around the fireplace, a determined look flashing in her eyes. "That woman is going down."

"I don't think the woman should be at the top of our suspect list," I said.

"If not her, it could be a Lynch rellie." Biddy perched on the edge of the couch cushion. "Noah showed up not long after you contacted Tommy's cousin. He hadn't seemed interested in his connection to Pringle, but maybe he told someone else who was. Maybe there *is* a big inheritance you know nothing about, and the person wants to keep Andrew from getting it."

"That's a bit farfetched," I said.

"Farfetched?" Biddy scoffed. "Just saw a movie with that exact plot. The bad guy killed off his nephew to keep the inheritance for himself. Could be one of Tommy's rellie's saw the same movie."

Gretta slapped a hand to her chest.

"That's probably not the case here," Biddy said.

Yet it reminded me of the Brendan Quigley mystery. The kidnapping and attempted murder of Collin's brother, Aidan, all over the inheritance of an unpublished manuscript.

"I do like the idea that he's in witness protection the best and it's the bad guys looking for him," Biddy said. "Like the mob or a drug cartel."

"What if he's on the run and scared for his life?" Gretta chewed on nail.

"Let's stay positive," Biddy said. "That it's a rellie trying to off him."

Gretta's gaze dimmed. "It's my cousin Millie."

"Hold off contacting her," I said. "If she's behind all of this, we don't want to let on that we know."

My gut told me that it wasn't as simple as Cousin Millie or a crooked or determined cop trying to skirt the system. That it was something more sinister.

It was time to step up our search for M.R. Pringle.

It was unlikely that whoever was looking for the guy was savvy enough to be monitoring his posts on genealogy forums from six months ago. Even though Gretta had promised Tommy not to contact Andrew, this was a matter of life and death. Besides, I wouldn't reveal my connection to Gretta.

After Gretta and Biddy left, I called Collin. I left a voice-mail that Biddy knew something was up and he'd better be smoothing things over by taking her to Paris.

I once again located Andrew's posts and replied that I might have information on the Bodkin relations he was researching. A vague comment would help ensure a response. If he hadn't turned on notifications for replies to his post, I wasn't sure of my next step.

# Eight

I STOPPED AT ROSIE'S, feeling bad that our visit hadn't ended on a cheery note the other day, thanks to Gretta. It would also be a nice break from searching for Gretta's grandson and my missing Christmas gift. I wouldn't mention that Gretta had volunteered Biddy and me to help decorate the gingerbread castle and that she might also be calling on Rosie for assistance.

I sat on Rosie's blue comfy living room chair, surrounded by calming gray walls and Christmas decor, sipping Irish breakfast tea. Edmond and Rosie sat across from me on the couch.

"Saw your post on the community alert page," Edmond said. "Have ya had any luck locating your package?"

I shook my head.

"Who nicks personalized items and doesn't return them?" Rosie said. "What's the chance you be knowing a golfer with the same initials?"

"Sadly, many people don't care about that," Edmond said.

"Your father and Ian staying with you is the biggest gift they could wish for, luv," Rosie said. "They'll be grand and certainly understand. Speaking of gifts." She walked to the towering Christmas tree and removed two vintage hand-blown glass ornaments—a red frosted bell and a brightly decorated tree. "My father traveled to Germany for work and always brought back lovely ornaments. These are two of my favorites." She handed them to me.

I studied the detailed craftmanship. "They're beautiful."

"They're yours." Rosie smiled.

"Thank you, but I can't take your favorite ornaments."

Word of my pathetic tree was apparently making the rounds.

"You're like a granddaughter to me. One day I want you to have them all. I need to know they're going to a good home."

We both teared up, and I gave Rosie a hug. "Thank you."

"Sorry I have no ornaments to be passing down, luv," Edmond said. "My Emily wasn't much for trees. You're still like a granddaughter to me though." He gave me a hug.

We sat back down and had tea, recovering from the emotional moment.

"Edmond mentioned you took the holidays off from genealogy work. You need some rest after all the publicity from that skeleton and the TV episode, not to mention that ghost busters' video. Will be good to have a relaxing holiday with family."

"I'm not officially working, just helping a friend with some genealogy research." I heaved a sigh, feeling over-whelmed.

"Not going well, is it?" Edmond asked.

I shrugged. "Only clue is the surname Bodkin. Never even heard of the name before."

"It's quite an uncommon one," Rosie said. "Was Sean's biological name."

I'd learned about her son Sean's adoption when I was helping Finn O'Brien identify his biological father. It turned out Sean wasn't Finn's father despite having been quite a womanizer...

Holy cats! Was Sean the father of Gretta's grandson?

*Rosie's* grandson?

Would make sense why nobody in the area was familiar with the surname Bodkin. Sean's adopted name was Connolly.

My mind raced while Rosie reminisced about the time Sean, an airline pilot, had taken her and her late husband on a trip to Portugal.

How old would Sean have been when he'd possibly had an affair with Maeve? Maeve was around Ita's age, early fifties. Sean would have been maybe four or five years older, so twenty-two when she was eighteen. Even if they hadn't gone to school together, it was a small community. They'd have had plenty of opportunities to come across each other. Had he been married to nasty Stella at the time?

"That sounds like it was a lovely trip," Edmond said, placing a hand on Rosie's.

She smiled. "Indeed it was. Stella hadn't joined us."

"Did Sean go to school with my mom?" I asked.

"He'd have been a few years older," Rosie said. "They surely knew each other."

Sean being the father of Maeve's baby would be a good

thing, except for the fact Sean was dead and Andrew would never have the chance to meet him. First, it wouldn't be splitting up a marriage and destroying a family or our close-knit community. Second, Rosie would make a wonderful grandmother. Third, an heir might trump Stella receiving the family estate.

A few months ago I'd warned Rosie that I'd discovered her daughter-in-law planned to go against Sean's wishes and sell the family estate to fund her retirement in the Canary Islands. Rosie had driven straight over to Stella's and threatened to disinherit her. Stella had gone psycho on poor Rosie. Sadly, it'd turned out there was nothing Rosie could do about the inheritance. Her husband, Patrick, had signed off in agreement with Sean that the estate would go to Stella after Patrick and Rosie passed away, if Sean was no longer living.

Yet was there a clause should Sean have an heir?

Could Biddy's farfetched movie theory be right?

Or maybe I just really wanted Stella to be guilty.

But what if Stella was behind the GenDNA scheme? She could have been trying to scare off Gretta by making her believe her grandson was a wanted criminal to keep her from discovering Sean's son, in line for the inheritance once Rosie passed away. I'd been convinced Stella had run Finn off the road, attempting to kill him to keep her inheritance when she'd thought he was Sean's son. The GenDNA scheme would be nothing compared to attempted murder, which Stella might be capable of.

"Do you think I should make them or not?" Rosie asked, jarring me from visions of Stella behind bars.

"That'd be great." I hadn't a clue what I was giving an opinion on.

"That's grand," Edmond said. "I fancy brussels sprouts."

I despised brussels sprouts. If I didn't focus on the conversation, I'd be agreeing to lamb. I was also here to smooth things over after Gretta's rude and distracted behavior. Still, I had the urge to spring from my chair and go tell Gretta my possible discovery!

Rosie began discussing one day visiting Brussels...

If Sean had a DNA account, Stella surely knew his email address and could have updated the account's password if not known. Was DNA how Sean had learned the identity of his biological parents and last name Bodkin? Or was Stella devious enough to have gotten his DNA test without his knowledge? *Here, honey, spit in this tube so I can have your cholesterol tested.* Asking Rosie if Sean had taken a DNA test would raise suspicion while we were on the topic of me trying to track down a Bodkin. Besides, Sean might have identified his parents by having his adoption records opened. If that was possible in Ireland.

I needed to find out if Sean's will mentioned an heir.

"Are you thinking about your father's and Ian's gifts, luv?" Rosie's question jarred me once again.

*No, I'm thinking you might be a grandmother!*

Yet what if she wasn't?

Besides, I couldn't tell Rosie without Gretta's approval. If Sean ended up not being the father, Gretta's secret would be out. That was a chance we might have to take. This could be the clue we needed to prove Andrew was indeed Maeve's child and not one of Gretta's sons' child.

I smiled and focused back on the conversation. Fifteen minutes and I'd be off to Gretta's.

I called Gretta from my car while still in Rosie's drive and discovered Tommy was gone. I told her I'd be right over. I was about to pull out when my phone rang. Noah.

"The fella emailed back. Refuses to ring me. He agreed to be exchanging emails tomorrow night, half six."

Of course the person wouldn't talk on the phone. That'd help us determine his nationality, age, and other identifying details. Why would he wait until tomorrow night and not want to know what Noah had to say ASAP? After all, he'd hired Noah and had him impersonating a police detective within twenty-four hours of Gretta appearing as Pringle's match.

"No worries though," he said. "My pal is working on getting the location for the IP address. Might be able to figure out the person's name and address."

"How's he doing that?"

"I'm not at liberty to divulge that information."

As if a computer hacker would even begin to compare with a forger, kidnapper, murderer, and other degenerates I'd encountered over the past year.

"That's fine. You need to do the emailing at my house so I can monitor your exchange." And make sure Noah didn't blow it. "We'll let the guy think you know the identity and location of Gretta's supposed half-sibling match. That Gretta has a few questions before she shares the information with him. Be here by six to prepare."

"That's grand. I'm off at five."

Even if Noah's buddy pinpointed the IP location, the address might have been rerouted, or it might have been a random location and the bad guy just happened to have been passing through Holyhock. It wouldn't be worth my time and money to fly over to Scotland and skulk around the Holyhock IP address area waiting to discover the person's identity.

However, it'd only be about an hour drive for Ian. He seemed intrigued by genealogy and my mystery solving. Perhaps he'd like to do a bit of sleuthing himself...

I hadn't told Gretta about coming across the name Bodkin last night, since I'd failed to find a local familiar with anyone by the name. And M.R. Pringle, like Cousin Millie, might not have a clue about genealogy research. I'd figured he might be way off on assuming he had a Bodkin connection.

But I had to share the info with Gretta now.

Gretta was sitting in the dark in her yellow living room. Even the Christmas tree lights weren't twinkling. She appeared groggy. Apparently she'd popped an antianxiety or sleep med after discovering Noah wasn't a legit detective and a bad guy might be after her grandson. And her cousin Millie might be the bad guy. Yet Gretta wasn't grasping what I was trying to tell her about the Bodkin connection.

I once again recounted my visit with Rosie.

Gretta stared at me through slitty lids. "Was a nice lad, Sean. I always thought Rosie's last name was Connolly."

"It is Connolly. Sean was adopted. His biological name was Bodkin."

"Ah, right, then." She nodded, but the light wasn't going

on. Gretta massaged her forehead, struggling to sort out my confusing story.

"Sean might be the father of Maeve's son," I blurted. "When I told Rosie I was researching the name Bodkin, she mentioned that was Sean's biological surname. She might have access to his adoption records or DNA account."

Gretta's eyes widened, and she nodded. "I *knew* the father was a married man. When I insisted Maeve marry the man if she wanted to keep the baby, that she could never raise a wee one on her own, she admitted he was already married. I'd pitched a fit and thrown her out of the house. Told her she wasn't allowed back home unless the child was given up for adoption. What an awful thing to have done when Maeve was straight out of school and had nowhere to turn. She was alone."

"Do you know of any connection Maeve and Sean might have had through work, school, or organizations?"

Gretta shook her head. "He'd have been at least three or four years older. No common interests that I know of. They certainly would have come across each other now and again."

"Someone in Sean's Bodkin family may have had contact with your grandson if they've taken a DNA test. DNA will be the only way to determine if Sean was indeed the father."

"We need to tell Rosie." Gretta sprang to her feet, throwing herself off balance. She grabbed the end table, and a white lamp wobbled on top. I dashed over and balanced her before it was the gingerbread castle all over again. At least she hadn't reached for the ornament-filled tree.

"Not sure how Rosie will feel about this," Gretta said. "She doesn't much care for me."

"I don't think that's true. I feel like things have gotten

better since you two worked together on the skeleton mystery."

Gretta nodded faintly. "If it turns out Sean's not the baby's father, Rosie will be privy to Maeve's secret and that I've taken a DNA test. It doesn't seem right for her to know before Maeve does. Yet I don't see any other choice. We might be running out of time as far as my grandson's safety is concerned."

Especially if Stella was involved. Biddy's idea of a drug cartel gave me a warm fuzzy feeling compared to the idea of nasty Stella being after Andrew. I wasn't telling either Rosie or Gretta my theory about Stella. They'd drive straight over to her Drumcara convenience store and confront the woman. The element of surprise was critical if *I* confronted Stella.

Edmond had left before we arrived at Rosie's. Gretta and I sat on the couch across from her in a chair. Thankfully, Gretta's meds hadn't fully worn off. She was patiently sipping tea, allowing me to take the lead instead of blurting out our sensitive news. Her subdued state should make for a more pleasant visit with Rosie than the last one.

"The friend I mentioned, who I'm assisting with genealogy research, is actually Gretta," I told Rosie.

Gretta's head snapped back in surprise. "Referred to me as a friend, did you?"

"Of course," I said.

A pleased smile curled the woman's thin lips.

"That's kind of you to assist her," Rosie said.

I eased out a breath. "I don't know if you recall hearing

that Gretta's daughter Maeve put a baby up for adoption in 1991."

Rosie's brow creased in contemplation. "I don't believe so."

"Gretta took a DNA test, hoping to connect with her grandson, and received the results a few days ago."

"Ah, that's lovely, isn't it now?" Rosie smiled at Gretta, likely realizing the reason for Gretta's rude and impatient behavior the other day. "I do hope you find the lad."

"We believe we have," I said. "We haven't made contact with him, but he posted on a few genealogy forums that he believes his paternal surname is Bodkin, which is an uncommon name."

Rosie nodded. "Indeed it is." She turned to Gretta. "Was my son Sean's biological..." Her gaze darted to me, her eyes widening. "You believe my Sean might be the lad's father?"

"We can't say for sure. I was hesitant to mention it because he might not even be *Maeve's* child. Could possibly be the child of one of Gretta's sons. Also, the name Bodkin is most common in Galway, where Maeve's brothers went to the university. And the baby's father might be one of their friends."

Rosie looked overwhelmed trying to process the information. "That would be a big coincidence, wouldn't it?"

I shrugged. "Family research is full of coincidences. Precisely why it's often hard to determine fact from fiction."

"I believe Sean was the father," Gretta piped up, nodding reassuringly. "I can feel it."

Rosie placed trembling fingertips to her lips, her eyes watering. "What a Christmas miracle. To have a connection to Sean. If only he were alive. He'd always wanted children."

Her gaze darkened. "It was Stella who didn't. He'd once come here quite upset and confided in me that she'd been on birth control for years when she'd supposedly been trying to conceive. She's a devious person." Rosie shook off her anger. "The lad will certainly be disappointed that his father's dead." She fidgeted with the strand of pearls around her neck. "What if he's not interested in knowing me because we aren't blood relations?"

"Blood isn't thicker than water," Gretta said. "Of course he'll be wanting to learn about his father and the parents, biological or not, who raised him. You're the finest woman I know. You'll be the biggest blessing to that child. So don't be talking nonsense."

A tear trailed down Rosie's cheek. "Thank you," she muttered, snatching a napkin from the tea service tray and drying her eyes.

Gretta blinked back tears. "Well, it's true. I pray that the lad was brought up by parents as wonderful as his father's."

Interesting that both Sean and Andrew were adopted.

A genealogist's nightmare.

"And he'll be fortunate to have such a strong woman and role model as yourself in his life," Rosie said.

"Not to be negative," I said, "but please remember there's the possibility he's not Sean's son."

Rosie nodded. "Sean married in February 1991. When was the lad born?"

"That July," Gretta said. "When Maeve had said the baby's father was married, maybe he hadn't been when the wee one was conceived. Merely engaged. And she mightn't have known about the pregnancy until after he married."

"Couldn't have blamed him for having an affair with a

wife like Stella," Rosie said. "And divorce wasn't legalized until the mid-nineties. Even once it was, it wasn't easy to obtain one. Wonder if Sean ever heard the rumor about Maeve's pregnancy."

"Maybe they were in love, and I'd forced Maeve to go to England and give the baby up for adoption." Gretta pressed her lips together, stifling a sob.

"Don't be blaming yourself," Rosie said. "Might merely have been a night of passion. Sean was a handsome fella and Maeve a lovely girl." Rosie gazed out a large picture window at the green fields and rolling hills, where sheep and cows had once grazed. "God only knows why it was Sean's wish this would all be Stella's." She frowned. "Now it can all belong to Sean's son. If it's indeed his son."

"The will provides for an heir?" I asked.

Rosie nodded. "Everything would go to an heir. I'd understand if he doesn't wish to keep the land, as this would all come as a complete shock to him. Yet he should inherit the estate and do as he please with it. Even if that means selling it."

Now knowing that Andrew would inherit the place, I'd be paying my buddy Stella a visit. It wouldn't be a joyous reunion after I'd accused her of murder at Finn's fake wake, especially when Finn hadn't actually been dead. Not to mention she likely figured I'd blabbed to Rosie about her plan to sell the estate and move to the Canary Islands despite Sean's wishes.

"Does the lad live in Ireland?" Rosie asked.

I shrugged. "We believe in Scotland, but not sure."

"What's his name?"

"Andrew," Gretta said. "At least we believe it's Andrew."

"Andrew," Rosie muttered. "What a fine name."

"Had Sean learned his biological surname from his adoption records or a DNA test?" I asked.

"A DNA test. I've met the Bodkins."

Gretta and I exchanged excited glances.

"After taking the DNA test, Sean hired a genealogist to figure it all out since he hadn't a clue how it worked. He'd had no close matches. The genealogist determined the Bodkins were his parents through a second-cousin match without having to contact the person."

What were the chances Stella hadn't known Sean had found his birth parents through a DNA test? Following his death or after Rosie threatened her inheritance, Stella might have monitored his account like a hawk in case an heir one day appeared and her inheritance *disappeared*. She could have deactivated Sean's account upon seeing Gretta matched his son. Actually, wouldn't she have deactivated Sean's account the day M.R. Pringle showed as a match, not wanting the guy showing *up* at her door?

"Did you and Sean meet his parents together?" I asked.

"Sadly, no. He had the test done a year before he passed away. He'd still been trying to decide whether or not to reach out to the Bodkins at the time of his death. I met them after he died. A lovely couple. They live in Offaly, or at least they had at the time. Even though they hadn't met him, I felt they had the right to know he'd passed. And it helped me to have a connection to his natural parents at such a sad time. Also, Sean having died of a rare heart condition, I felt they deserved to know in case they weren't aware it might run in the family." She gasped. "I certainly hope Sean's son hasn't inherited it."

"Jesus, Mary, and Joseph," Gretta muttered. "I hope not."

"Would be nice for him to have the medical history." I needed to obtain Ian's. Yet he'd surely have mentioned anything life threatening. "Could you contact the Bodkins and see if they know the second-cousin relation who'd taken the DNA test?"

"I can certainly ring them to arrange a visit. The news would be best given in person. At the time I met them, they hadn't told their family about Sean. That may complicate matters. Can't imagine they wouldn't have contacted me if they already knew about Sean's son."

The couple was the lead we needed to confirm Andrew was Maeve's child.

"There's something else you need to know about." I filled Rosie in on Noah having been hired to play the detective role. "We don't know why someone is searching for him."

Rosie's gaze darkened. "I'll ring the Bodkins straight away. I'm sure they're busy with the holidays. I'll promise to make it a quick visit. With any luck, they're home." She left to make the call in private and returned minutes later. "Had to leave a voicemail."

Gretta and I heaved impatient sighs.

"Please don't be mentioning this to anyone," Gretta said. "Not until we know more."

"Of course not. However, I must tell Edmond. I couldn't keep something like this from him."

Gretta nodded. "Wouldn't expect you to. I should have told Tommy sooner. He's still coming to terms with me having taken the test without his or Maeve's blessing and how telling Maeve will affect our family. I promised not to contact the lad until I've spoken with Maeve. If we determine he is Maeve's child, I plan to tell her when she's over for the New Year. No sense saying a word until then."

If DNA didn't identify the baby's father, would Maeve?

# Nine

ON THE WAY to Stella's convenience store in Drumcara, I brought Biddy up to speed on Rosie possibly being Andrew's grandmother and my theory about Stella being our mystery *man*.

Biddy smiled proudly. "Right, then. My theory about a rellie tracking down Andrew to kill him before he could claim an inheritance isn't so mad after all, is it now?"

"It's only a theory at this point. And Stella isn't going to crack easily. We need to be subtle. Can't be accusing her of anything and putting her on the defense."

"What's your plan?" Biddy asked.

"Follow my lead."

I had no lead. I hadn't a clue how to approach Stella without raising suspicion, especially when she likely wasn't speaking to us. Hopefully, the store's tasty latte jump-started my creative juices. And regifting Stella a box of chocolates from my cupboard might help break the ice.

A white sign greeted us at Drumcara's village limits—the town's name in both English and Gaelic. I parked in the lot, and my heart raced as we entered the store. Stella, a blond middle-aged woman, stood behind the counter chatting with a customer, oblivious to our arrival. Based on her heavily tanned skin and brassy blond hair, she'd been spending time in the Canary Islands.

Biddy and I breezed back to the coffee machine. Heart thumping, I dispensed a steaming latte into a paper cup, scrambling for ideas on how to approach the nasty woman. Biddy held my cup while I grabbed two family-size packages of lasagna from the prepared-food section, for Christmas Eve dinner. The deli ham looked sketchy, but I scored two cans of sliced pineapple. A nice dent in my holiday grocery shopping.

The customer left, and we headed to the counter.

Stella spotted us approaching and rolled her eyes. "Will that be all?" Her gravelly voice reminded me of Cousin Millie. She started ringing up our groceries.

My palms sweated. "In the spirit of Christmas, I brought you a gift." I set the box of chocolates on the counter.

Her suspicious gaze narrowed on the candy.

"It's sweets, not a bloody bomb." Biddy smiled sweetly. "Speaking of treats, I should be grabbing some crisps while we're here. Hope ya have Pringles. I fancy the salt and vinegar ones." She eyed Stella. "What do you think of *Pringles*?"

So much for being subtle and following my lead.

Stella didn't bat an eyelash. "Crisps are down the first aisle on the left."

"I really shouldn't be snacking." Biddy gave her flat stomach a pat. "Think I've gained a stone from too many biscuits already this season. Yet life is short. Shouldn't be putting things off, should ya? Like eating your favorite crisps or getting married and having children. Or *not* having children and later regretting it."

"Did you and Sean have children?" I asked innocently.

Stella glared at me, her features hardening. "You know darn well we were never blessed with children. It wasn't meant to be. And don't come in here trying to act all nice in the spirit of Christmas when you tried to frame me for murder and told Rosie a bunch of lies hoping I'd lose my inheritance." With a crazed look on her face, the woman leaned across the counter toward us, and we snapped back. "She can't take it away. It's mine, and there's not a thing she can do about it." A devious smile curled her dry lips. "Not. A. Thing." She slammed a fist down on the box of chocolates, crushing it.

Heart racing, I nudged Biddy, who was paralyzed with fear. I grabbed the change and groceries, and we bolted out the shop. I took several calming breaths as we headed toward my car.

"She's totally guilty," I said.

"And psycho. A scary combination. And now she knows we're onto her. I'm starting to hope she's not guilty and merely hates our guts."

If she was guilty, would our confrontation make her back off or motivate her to find Andrew, kill him, and secure her inheritance?

"When I was trying to identify Finn's father, I didn't trust her one bit. I caught her in several lies, and it was obvious she hadn't cared for her husband. I'd suspected she might have been responsible for offing Sean besides trying to kill Finn."

"Yet if she's here working, she can't be in Scotland sending emails."

"Could have hired someone to do the dirty work. Even though she probably enjoys doing her own dirty work."

"Would she be smart enough to know about rerouting an IP address? We hadn't a clue."

"Easy enough to have hired someone like Noah's friend to do it."

"If she did reroute it, why to Scotland? Is Holyhock just a random location that means nothing? If it means *something*, what could it be?"

"Who knows." Probably Stella. I peered through the store window at her and a lady laughing, whereas Biddy and I were still recovering from our traumatic encounter.

Was she guilty, or did we just bring out the worst in the woman?

❧ ❧

I pulled into Biddy's driveway around back of the pub.

She reached for the door handle, then paused. "Collin is still acting strange. I'm thinking I need to be breaking up with him before he breaks up with me."

"Seriously?" I shrieked. "This isn't junior high. You don't break up with a guy because you think he's breaking up with you. Because the guy passed a note to Suzy Rankin and you thought he had the hots for her when actually he was wondering what to get you for your birthday." I snapped my mouth shut, afraid she thought the birthday reference was about Collin and her Christmas present.

Biddy looked at me like I'd gone mad. "Didn't say I was doing it for sure. Just considering it."

She stepped from the car, and I phoned Collin. The call went to voicemail, and my grip tightened around the phone. I told him if he didn't take Biddy to Paris, I was getting his coworker's name and offering to cat sit for his sister. Biddy and I'd go to Paris and find some hot French guys!

When I arrived at home, I hung Rosie's glass ornaments on the tree, which wasn't looking nearly as sad as it had a few days ago. The three ornaments I'd bought during my travels gave me the idea of having one made for Dalwade Castle. What a perfect memento for guests to have from their stay at the historical castle hotel. I'd have to mention that to Archie.

Rosie called to confirm our visit with the Bodkins the next day. They lived about an hour away in County Offaly. Fingers crossed the couple would be the clue we needed to confirm Sean was Andrew's father.

I stuck the lasagna in the freezer next to several individual store-bought meals. Tomorrow when I stopped at my favorite petrol station for gas, the prepared-foods section had better be well stocked. I made tea and sat on the couch with a peanut butter cookie.

The doorbell rang. Gretta. She marched inside the house with a determined look.

"Rosie contacting the Bodkins has me thinking about the fact that I never properly thanked Tommy's cousin, Marion Marshall, for taking Maeve in and helping her through the pregnancy and adoption. Not only was I an awful mother to Maeve during her time of need, I was unappreciative to the Marshalls. It certainly isn't doing my karma any good. I need to be making amends. Need to tell them how much I appreciate what they did. If they hadn't taken Maeve in, she might have ended up in a shelter for unwed mothers or on the street." Gretta choked back tears. "Maeve thought leaving her friends behind to temporarily live in England was another form of punishment. Yet afterward she returned home for barely a year before putting the Irish Sea between us once again." She eased out a shaky breath. "I must apologize and thank them properly for all they did."

I placed a comforting hand on Gretta's arm. "That's a great idea. Christmas is the perfect time to make amends."

"I can't do it at home with Tommy there. Maeve is still a sensitive topic for him. Would it be okay if I rang them from here?"

I nodded. "Of course."

Gretta dropped down onto the love seat. I tried to focus on my computer and not her conversation.

"No, I'm not dying," Gretta told Tommy's cousin Marion. "Just been wanting to thank you properly for years." She gave her eyes an exasperated roll, as if to say *Why does everyone think I must be dying to want to make amends?*

Gretta and the woman chatted, catching up on the past six years. Fifteen minutes into the conversation, Gretta waved a hand frantically in the air, getting my attention.

Her eyes widened. "So Bernie retired after fifty years, did he? Guess I never knew the name of his employer was *Pringle* and Company. Merely knew he worked in the woolen goods industry in England."

My heart raced.

Pringle was a *company* name, not merely a *surname*?

More importantly, it'd been Bernie's employer.

"How lovely they had an office in Manchester when

they're based out of Scotland. Where are they headquartered in Scotland?" Gretta's eyes grew wider. "Holyhock?"

Holy cats!

Was Andrew connected to Pringle & Company, the surname, or both? Had a coworker of Bernie's adopted Maeve's son? A member of the family-owned company?

Could be it was merely a coincidence since the name originated in that area hundreds of years ago and there might still be tons of Pringles in County Roxburgshire.

Five minutes later, Gretta politely ended the call and promised to stay in touch. Hand trembling, she slipped her phone into her purse. "Pringle and Company is a woolen goods manufacturer. What if it's a family-owned company? Is Andrew part of that Pringle family? Or one of his parents worked with Bernie?"

"If it was a coworker who adopted your grandson, I don't know how we'd go about determining the person's identity unless it was a member of the Pringle family and Andrew's last name is indeed Pringle. But I've searched for Andrew Pringles and come up empty."

"If Andrew's father worked there, maybe the lad works there also. Maybe that's not his last name but instead his employer's name."

"Maybe M.R. is his work position or credentials. I could search professional networking sites for Andrews who work at Pringle and Company. How does the IP address in Holyhock and the mystery man work into all of this? Did his search for Andrew lead him to Holyhock, where he hit a dead end? Or is he a Pringle employee? Then why not look in the company directory to find Andrew?"

Gretta looked like her head was spinning as fast as mine.

"I best be going. Tommy will be wondering what I'm up to so late." She pressed her hand against her forehead. "Think I could use another one of those antianxiety meds. My heart is racing."

"I'll do some research tonight and see what I can find."

Gretta left, and I got to work.

According to the Pringle & Company's website, their headquarters was located just outside Holyhock. Besides woolen goods, they were a holding company for a fashion clothing chain and a home goods store. The three companies combined employed over thirty thousand people. The fashion clothing company headquartered in Wales had 503 stores throughout the UK and Europe. Andrew could work for any of the three companies under any last name.

An hour later, I'd polished off my last rosette and a glass of mulled wine. I'd been searching the internet like a mad woman. I learned M.R. in the corporate world could stand for numerous positions, such as market research. According to professional networking sites, at least thirty-two Andrews and nickname variations worked for the three Pringle-owned companies. Not one Andrew Pringle. I was becoming more certain that Andrew's last name wasn't Pringle. That he worked for the company.

A text dinged on my phone. Noah. *The IP address is for a Mungo's restaurant in Holyhock.*

Maybe the restaurant was located near where the mystery person lived or worked. Like at Pringle's headquarters. Or he'd just been passing through town and stopped for a cup of coffee on a long drive back to MI6 headquarters in London. And it was all a coincidence.

I thanked Noah and his friend for illegally obtaining the

IP address. Good to know that figuring one out wasn't easy. My list of sketchy acquaintances just kept growing.

I called Ian and told him about my new Pringle clue. I filled him in on the mystery man and Noah not being a detective. My numerous theories on the bad guy's involvement and why he was possibly searching for Andrew. How I'd set up a sting operation to take place between Noah and the guy tomorrow night because I feared for Andrew's safety.

"I could give Mungo's restaurant a visit tomorrow night and see if a dodgy-looking character is typing away on a device. Could also pay a visit to Pringle and Company and ask if Andrew Pringle is available and see if I hit the jackpot."

Getting Ian involved and possibly putting his life at risk made me nervous.

"Might be a shop or pub across the street you could hang out in and see if anyone suspicious goes into Mungo's. Don't confront the person. We don't know how dangerous he might be."

Ian chuckled. "Never thought my daughter would one day be giving *me* safety tips."

Daughter...

Awkward silence filled the line.

"How were you able to determine an IP address location?" he asked.

"You don't want to know."

"Aye. That's what I was afraid of."

Computer hacker was low on my list of dodgy people I'd encountered since moving to Ireland. Who knew what I was up against now?

We said goodbye.

It felt weird that I was confiding in Ian and hadn't

mentioned anything to Dad. It could make the Christmas holiday a bit awkward if Ian and I were discussing a mystery Dad knew nothing about. And I hadn't been the best daughter lately, not staying in touch. Following Mom's death, Dad had sold the house and moved to his parents' condo in Florida, which he'd inherited. He'd made the choice to leave my sisters and his friends in Chicago, but I still worried he was lonely.

Dad picked up on the second ring.

"You just caught me," he said, short of breath. "Meeting up with a friend at the golf club, then going to see the play, *A Christmas Carol*. Haven't seen it in years. Probably since we took you and your sisters when you were in grade school."

"That sounds fun. Who's your friend?"

"Charlie. It's not a date, if that's what you're wondering."

"Just asking. But since you brought it up..."

"And I'm dropping it."

Dad hadn't dated since Mom's death. Not that I was aware of anyway. At least I felt better that he wasn't at home lying on the couch watching *Miracle on 34th Street*—Mom's favorite movie—while eating an entire box of fudge and drinking brandy slushes.

He put me on speakerphone in his SUV. I brought him up to speed on my crazy life.

"Too bad I wasn't there," he said. "I could meet up with Ian and play Hardy Boys. I shouldn't make light of the situation. You be careful."

"I told Ian the same thing, and he said, 'Never thought my daughter would one day be giving *me* safety tips.'"

Silence filled the line.

"The word *daughter* slipped out and was a bit awkward for both of us." Just like it was now.

"I'm glad to hear you two are getting on." Dad sounded sincere, yet a bit off. My comment had thrown him.

We chatted a few more minutes about random things, avoiding the topic of Ian. We hung up, and I dropped back against the couch, hoping my *daughter* comment didn't make the holiday uncomfortable for the three of us. Not when Dad and Ian had been getting along so well.

Great. Now I was more worried about Dad's relationship with Ian than my own!

# Ten

In County Offaly, Biddy parked behind a silver compact SUV in the Bodkins' drive. The whitewashed stone house with a red door and window trim was an hour drive from Ballycaffey. An LED candle lit in each window welcomed visitors. Before we could ring the bell, Imelda Bodkin greeted us at the door. In her early seventies, she had shoulder-length silver hair and was dressed in a red cashmere sweater and tan slacks. She escorted us into a light-green sitting room, where her husband, Owen, was throwing peat into a woodstove. A tall man, he was bald with a thick gray beard and mustache. His handsome appearance reminded me of Sean Connery, but his soft brown eyes with thick lashes resembled those of Sean *Connelly*, Rosie's son. At least from the photos I'd seen.

After ten minutes of pleasantries and tea, Rosie took the lead. "I'm not sure how else to say this." She gazed between the couple. "I think Sean and Gretta's daughter Maeve may have had a son. Gretta took a DNA test and discovered her grandson. Can't say for sure, but he believes he has a connection to the surname Bodkin."

Imelda and her husband exchanged surprised glances.

"Might you ask him the names of some matches?" she said. "They'd likely be distant relations, but I might know if there's a connection. Like with the second cousin you told me had helped the genealogist identify us."

Gretta explained her sensitive situation with Maeve and the promise she'd made to her husband to not contact Andrew. She left out the part that her grandson wasn't accepting messages.

"It'd be helpful to confirm if Sean is or isn't the lad's father," Rosie said. "If Andrew is Sean's son, the lad deserves to know the cause of this father's death and his medical background."

Imelda nodded. "We were quite surprised to hear how Sean had died. After some research we learned that Owen's great-uncle had also suffered from a rare heart condition. The man lived in Italy, so we'd never met him, and the information wasn't passed along in the family."

"Italy?" Biddy and I blurted out.

The woman nodded. "Owen's grandfather emigrated from northern Italy."

"The lad has ten percent Italian ethnicity," Gretta said.

Imelda nibbled on her lower lip. "We still haven't told our children about Sean. Only sixteen when I became pregnant, I was sent to live with relations in Donegal. We were much too young to have given him a good life. Years later we were blessed with two more children, Ella and Niall, and three granddaughters." She smiled at Rosie. "We're thankful Sean had such wonderful parents who raised him."

"It might be time to tell the kids." Owen placed a hand on his wife's leg. "Keeping the past a secret no longer seems fair to Sean's memory. And it would be nice to get to know our grandson since we didn't have the chance to know Sean." He peered over at Rosie. "When you visited us after his death, we wished he'd have reached out to us but understood that he'd needed time to think about it. Just too bad he hadn't had enough time."

Owen phoned his second cousin, who he'd met at a family reunion. If the woman had contact with Andrew, she'd likely have reached out to the Bodkins. It turned out his cousin had taken a break from genealogy over the past year. She had him hold while she checked her Ancestry.com messages and found one from Andrew inquiring about their connection. His amount of shared DNA confirmed Sean was Andrew's father.

Owen asked her to respect their privacy and allow us to reach out to him. Not that she could anyway. Andrew was no longer accepting messages.

Rosie and Gretta burst into tears and wrapped each other in a warm embrace. Something I never dreamed would happen.

A Christmas present that meant more than a dozen personalized golf balls. I needed to get over the golf balls. Spending time with my dads over the holidays was priceless.

My *dads*. I'd always referred to them as Dad and Ian.

I couldn't imagine ever addressing Ian as Dad no matter how well we got along. It wouldn't feel right. The thought of slipping up and calling Ian Dad in front of Dad made me nervous.

We'd decided before arriving at the Bodkins not to share

the fact that Andrew's life might be in danger. The news of a grandson was overwhelming enough. No sense making them worry about his safety until we knew what was going on. Right now we had a better chance at locating Andrew than figuring out who was after him.

A crooked or even legit cop, Stella, and Cousin Millie were on my suspect list. If one of them rerouted the IP address to Holyhock, how had the person connected Andrew to the area or company? Perhaps he or she was familiar with Pringle & Company and had assumed his profile name was based on his job, not his surname. Even if Stella wasn't intelligent enough, she was devious enough to create the scheme. And Cousin Millie was greedy enough, but would she have the connections to do it?

Hopefully, my questions would be answered after Noah made contact with the mystery man tonight and Ian possibly identified him at Mungo's restaurant in Holyhock.

Pringle's headquarters was pretty much shut down for the holidays, so Ian didn't have luck finding an employee named Andrew Pringle. He was staking out Mungo's from a pub across the street. As far as he could tell, none of the restaurant's seven diners, including a family of four, were typing away on a laptop or other device. Just past 6:00 p.m., our mystery man likely hadn't yet arrived. However, *Noah* should have arrived at my house by now to prepare for the email exchange with the person.

"Where is that eejit?" Biddy glared out my living room window, dressed in a green Grinch sweatshirt. Appropriate attire. Thanks to Collin's suspicious behavior, her holiday spirit was fading fast. "He's probably lost. Couldn't find his way back home the other day without asking for directions. Too proud to call and ask ya for them now."

"Then he should be answering *my* calls."

Fifteen minutes later, Biddy was cruising the roads of Ballycaffey, searching for Noah while I paced the living room floor, talking to Ian. "If he's not here in time, he better pull off the road to email. If he screws this up, I'll shake him senseless, which won't take much shaking."

"Can I buy you a drink?" a woman's voice carried across the line. Not a waitress asking if she could *get* Ian a drink.

"Sorry. I'm here on business," Ian said.

"Getting hit on?"

"Aye, she's quite the bonnie lassie. Lovely auburn hair." He lowered his voice. "Not as lovely as Rhona, of course. She's sitting at the bar across from my table."

"Noah's lucky the guy hasn't showed up yet," I said.

"Hold on. This might be our bloke, wearing a dark suit. The past five minutes he's been standing down from the pub, leaning against a lamppost and peering over the top of a newspaper at the restaurant. Could be he's waiting to make sure he wasn't followed before going inside."

"Can you snap a pic in case it's him?"

"Aye. Will text it to you."

My phone dinged the arrival of the photo. A familiar-looking dark-haired guy in a black suit with gorgeous blue eyes peering out from behind a newspaper.

"That's Noah! I'm putting you on conference call and phoning him." I punched his number on speed dial.

"He glanced down at his mobile and stuffed it back in his jacket pocket."

I texted him. *Get your butt inside McGregor's pub. Now!*

"He read the message and is looking over here for ya," Ian said. "I gave him a wave. He's back behind the newspaper."

I texted again. *Now!!!!!!*

"He's heading toward the pub. Want to speak with him?"

"Oh yeah." My grip tightened around the phone while Ian put Noah on. "What are you doing in Scotland when you're supposed to be at my house?"

"Flights to Edinburgh are fierce cheap even with the holiday. Was only an hour flight. Decided to hop a plane this morning. Thought it'd be better if I email the fella that I'm here and know what he looks like. Figure he'll be looking around acting all nervous and give himself away. I'd take him down and be a hero."

"You've probably already scared him off skulking around the outside of Mungo's like some 1940s film noir detective. Not to mention we don't know he's going to contact you from the same spot. Now you're not here for me to monitor the email exchange. You're going to botch this up, if you haven't already."

"It was your fella here who blew my cover," Noah said.

"By getting you out of sight?" My voice squeaked in annoyance. I eased out a calming breath. "Okay. Keep talking on Ian's phone and email on yours so I can read you the script."

When the mystery man hadn't yet emailed at 6:35 p.m., I had Noah reach out to him. Time ticked by... Only the family of four remained in Mungo's. Had the mystery man been one of the three who'd left after spotting Noah skulking around outside? I should have had Ian take photos of anyone coming out of the restaurant, not merely going in it, but hadn't figured the guy would leave before making contact. I had Noah shoot the person another email. At 7:00 p.m. we finally gave up. Noah put Ian back on the phone.

"Why wouldn't he have made contact with Noah when he was desperate to know Andrew's identity and whereabouts?" My mind raced. "Unless he already learned both. Or Noah botched up the sting and the guy realized he was being setup."

Or it was Stella and she'd backed off after learning we were onto her.

"You came here without money for a hotel?" Ian said to Noah.

"Is that loser asking for a place to stay?" I said.

"Aye. The train from Edinburgh cost more than expected, and he doesn't have enough quid for a room."

"What would he have done if you two hadn't met up?"

"Haven't a clue. Neither does the cheeky laddie, I'm sure."

We said good night, and I tossed my phone onto the couch.

Unbelievable. Noah was staying at Ian's when I hadn't even stayed there. He was sneaking a peek into my biological father's personal life. His favorite decorating colors, furniture style, foods, Christmas cookies, books... I wished I'd accepted Ian's invite to Edinburgh for the Christmas market.

I hadn't told Gretta about the plan for fear she'd distract me or somehow mess things up, and it ended up being Noah. The wannabe detective flunky.

The front door slammed shut, and Biddy stalked into the

living room, having used her house key. "No sign of the gobshite. He's going to wish I'd found him on the side of the road with a flat tire when I see him. And I drove past Stella's shop. She wasn't working."

Had she been at home checking her emails from Noah?

I filled Biddy in on Noah showing up in Holyhock.

"What an eejit! And can't believe he's staying with Ian when you haven't even stayed with him."

I shrugged. "It's not a big deal."

Then why was I gritting my teeth and planning to interrogate Noah about his sleepover at Ian's as soon as he was on Irish soil?

Biddy left, and an hour later I was still trying to shake off my anger at Noah and desire to shake him senseless. I took a gulp of tea, which added to the heat raging through my body.

An email notification popped up that someone had replied to my comment on a genealogy forum. I hadn't posted to a forum outside of social media in eons.

Except for M.R. Pringle's surname post!

Heart racing, I opened the email and clicked through to his comment on the forum's website.

*Thanks for the response. Would appreciate whatever information you might have on my possible Bodkin relations.*

*Cheers, Andrew*

I drummed my fingers nervously against the keyboard. I couldn't reply for the entire world to see, including our MIA mystery man. I had a backup email address for when I preferred to remain anonymous or avoid online stalkers. It was highly doubtful that the bad guy was monitoring Andrew's forum posts from six months ago. And the guy wouldn't receive notifications of comments unless he'd commented. Mine had been the post's first response.

I stopped just shy of posting my alternate email address. Gretta had promised Tommy she wouldn't contact their grandson until she'd told Maeve. Technically, I'd already violated that promise with my initial comment on the forum. However, Gretta had made the promise. I hadn't.

I called Gretta and apologized for not telling her that I'd reached out to Andrew.

Silence filled the line.

"Are you there?" I asked.

"Yes," she muttered. "Can't believe he responded to your message. Read me his reply again."

I reread it several times. If I provided her with the forum's link, she could stay up all night reading the post. Yet Gretta might reach out to him and scare him off.

"Ah, that's lovely, isn't it now?" Her voice trembled, and I picture her fighting back tears. "The lad has great manners. Must have been raised in a proper home."

"I'm not comfortable responding to him until you've told Tommy and Maeve."

Gretta exhaled a shaky breath. "It's the right thing to do. I'll tell Tommy tonight and ring Maeve first thing in the morning. Will ring you after."

I wished her good luck.

A chill shot up my spine, and the hairs on the back of my neck stood at attention. Maeve was going to flip out. I didn't blame her. This was a difficult situation for everyone involved. Tomorrow morning might be the end of Tommy's and Gretta's relationship with their daughter. They'd have to live with their regrets over how they'd handled the delicate situation thirty-one years ago. And now.

Did Maeve live with the same regret? Perhaps she'd be happy that Gretta had taken the initiative to locate her son. Maybe she'd been unable to bring herself to do so, unsure if her son would accept her after all these years. Finding Andrew might repair the family's damaged relationship.

Regardless of the outcome, several people's lives were about to change. I hoped it was for the better.

# Eleven

MY PHONE RANG on the nightstand at 7:00 a.m. Gretta. I bolted upright in bed, snatching the phone from the table, nearly knocking off a pristine orange cloth-covered book with gold writing on the spine. *Letters, Queen Victoria, 1837-1861.*

"I spoke to Maeve last evening." Gretta sniffled. "Wasn't up to ringing ya after. It went as expected. I'm sure she'll never speak to me again. I only hope she takes it out on me and not Tommy."

"I'm sure that was difficult. How's Tommy doing?"

"Not well."

"Do you still want me to respond to Andrew?"

"Yes, please contact the lad. I've honored Tommy's wish of telling Maeve. We have to at least be warning him that someone is going to great lengths to find him. I didn't tell Maeve this, or that her son might be a wanted man. I couldn't. She hung up on me." Gretta choked back a sob. "I must be going."

Poor Gretta. Yet Maeve's reaction was no surprise.

I rolled out of bed and slipped the phone into the pocket of my flannel bottoms. I trudged down the spiral staircase in Berber slippers to the kitchen, where my laptop sat on the table. I made a double-bagged cup of tea and peered out the window into darkness. Too early for Pinky to be popping by for breakfast. I located Andrew's post and provided him my backup email address. I kept the message short and clicked the notification box.

I ate a flaky pastry. The delicious pastries were making me proud of my 5 percent Norwegian heritage. I refreshed my backup email website nonstop until his response popped up ten minutes later. He thanked me again for reaching out. He was curious what information I might have on his Bodkin relations.

My heart thumped in my ears.

I hadn't thought through precisely how I was going to approach the subject. It was Gretta and Rosie's place to provide him with his family history. While I was struggling to compile a response, he asked where I lived. When I said Ireland, he wondered if we could meet today in Dublin. My breath caught in my throat. That meant he was a short airplane flight, ferry ride, or drive away. I didn't want to scare him off by asking where he lived. I'd scare him off once I told him that somebody was looking for him.

What clandestine meeting place was halfway between the Dublin airport and seaport?

Glasnevin Cemetery. It was located in a northern suburb. The cemetery offered tours, a lovely café, and a gift shop. We'd never run into someone we knew there. At least not someone living. Better yet, I suggested The Gravediggers, a pub directly outside the cemetery's side gate. I'd been wanting to visit the place, and the crowd was certainly more cemetery tourists than locals.

Several minutes ticked by and he still hadn't responded.

He was undoubtedly questioning my suggestion, wondering if I had an ulterior motive for recommending the spot. Like I planned to lure him into the cemetery and shove him into an open grave. It was far from a deserted cemetery, like the ones Grandma and I'd often traipsed through. Grandma had once taken me to Glasnevin to tour the graves of Irish heroes. After recently tracing Grandpa Fitzsimmons's family tree, I learned I had a distant connection to Michael Collins, one of the most important heroes in Irish history. Visiting the man's grave would mean even more now.

Andrew finally replied he'd meet me there at 4:00 p.m. today.

Warning him to make sure he wasn't followed might freak him out. It worried me that the mystery man had no-showed last night. He went from desperately searching for Andrew to going MIA. Why would he stop his search unless he'd already found him? Yet the fact that I was communicating with Andrew told me he hadn't found him. Or at least he hadn't yet confronted, arrested, or murdered him.

I mentioned that I was bringing Gretta. That I didn't merely know information on his paternal Bodkin relations— I knew his mother's relations too. I left out that I was also bringing Rosie and Biddy, not wanting to overwhelm him. All three would insist on joining me. Unless Biddy had exceeded her cemetery quota for the year.

Andrew replied he welcomed the chance to meet his first blood relation. A sense of anticipation raced through me. I couldn't imagine how he was feeling.

A text dinged on my phone. Ian. *Just dropped the laddie off at the airport. Gave him twenty quid to eat.*

What a loser.

I thanked Ian and told him we were going to meet Andrew that afternoon.

*Good luck. Hope all goes grand.*

So did I.

Rosie and Gretta had insisted on leaving shortly after I'd phoned them. They feared we might run into holiday traffic, road construction, or an accident and it would take us eight hours rather than an hour to get to Glasnevin. An early departure was fine. Plenty of time for me to wander around the cemetery before meeting with Andrew. Gretta thought the cemetery was a brilliant idea, whereas Rosie thought it a bit morbid for a first meeting. Especially when we were going to have to break the news to Andrew that his father, Sean, was dead. Biddy wasn't thrilled about another cemetery. However, she was intrigued when I described the watch-towers around the perimeter, where men stood guard to protect graves against body snatchers. My nickname Tombstone Terminator would have been perfect for the guards.

Like me, Biddy had a morbid curiosity.

When I'd discovered the dead man on my grandparents' graves, she'd explained that stealing bodies had been a huge source of income for grave robbers in the 1800s. They'd sell the bodies to the growing number of medical schools. People protected their loved ones with inventions like grave guns, coffin torpedoes, and mortsafes—iron grids that covered the graves. Of course, I was familiar with body snatchers but hadn't realized it'd been such a prevalent and lucrative source of income.

It was misting when we arrived at the cemetery shortly before noon. Rosie and Gretta opted for tea in the cemetery's cozy café, while Biddy and I headed straight for a watch-tower. Sadly, the towers' doors were bricked off, preventing us from sneaking a peek inside one. A tower still provided a great photo op. I had my picture taken next to the graves of several Irish heroes, ending with Michael Collins. I bought a book on women heroes in Irish history buried there and a Michael Collins mug. We picked up Rosie and Gretta and headed over to The Gravediggers pub for a late lunch.

Fifteen minutes later, we were seated in a large wooden booth inside the pub. Biddy and I were wearing souvenir Gravedigger T-shirts. Not real festive, but they were green. We were perusing the menu when a pretty fiftyish-year-old woman with light-brown hair dressed in a red wool coat entered the pub.

Gretta gasped. "Maeve."

Biddy and I exchanged confused glances. Maeve?

Andrew was due there in an hour.

Apparently Maeve had a change of heart about joining Gretta and meeting her son. Yet she didn't look excited at the prospect of reuniting with him after thirty-one years.

Gretta's daughter marched toward us, her heels echoing against the wood floor. She came to an abrupt halt at the end of our booth. Biddy and I snapped back on our bench.

"Did Tommy tell you I was here?" Gretta fidgeted nervously with the Michael Collins keychain on the strap of her tan purse.

Maeve shook her head. "*Andrew* told me."

We all looked baffled.

"Andrew contacted me about your meeting him here today. He was thrilled, until of course I was forced to tell him the truth. That I'm his mother."

Gretta's gaze narrowed in confusion. "What are you saying?"

"Andrew's adopted father is a friend of Cousin Marion's husband, Bernie. They worked together. Despite you insisting I give my son up for adoption, I found a way to be in his life without him knowing I'm his mother, until now. Until you decided to ruin his life as well as mine one more time."

Gretta paled.

"Janey," Biddy muttered.

"Jesus, Mary, and Joseph." Rosie placed trembling fingers against her open lips.

Apparently Gretta had lied about telling Maeve she was searching for her son. Maeve would have confessed she'd long found him.

"Needless to say, he's angry and quite devastated. He'll likely never speak to me again. I hope you're satisfied."

"That was why you returned to England to live?" Gretta asked. "To be nearer your son? And Bernie and Marion knew this all along?"

Maeve nodded. "Six months ago Andrew took a DNA test to learn if he was 100 percent English and discovered he's mostly Irish and adopted. He contacted a match in Galway, who claimed her dead brother was his father. He became disheartened, and I offered to manage his account. I knew one day I'd have to admit the truth, with the growing popularity of DNA testing. I just had to figure out how. After a bit of research, I realized the woman was mad. She was too distant a relation to be his aunt. Then you showed up as a match a few days ago. I panicked, trying to figure out how to tell him."

Gretta looked sucker punched.

"So you also manage his GenDNA account?" I asked.

Maeve shot me a nasty look for interrupting her rant.

Gretta stared at her daughter in disbelief. "I wanted to help my grandson rather than once again abandoning him because he might be a wanted criminal. When we uncovered your cold-case scheme, I feared someone was hunting him down for malicious reasons rather than arresting him."

Maeve's forehead wrinkled in confusion.

Biddy sprang from the bench. "Can't believe ya made us think someone was trying to kill him. I have half a mind to turn ya in to the garda."

Maeve's gaze darted between Gretta and Biddy. "What are you going on about?"

Biddy stared her down. "Bet ya didn't tell Andrew about your scheme, did ya?"

"I haven't a clue what you're talking about." Maeve's confused expression turned to sheer panic. "What do you mean Andrew's in danger?"

Biddy and I exchanged skeptical looks.

"What do you mean?" Maeve demanded, slamming a hand against the table.

I recounted our visit from *Detective* Noah Kenny. That in the end we'd discovered he wasn't in law enforcement. That someone had hired him to find Andrew. Or to keep Gretta from finding her grandson. I didn't mention that last part or that I'd hoped Stella was guilty.

Since it now appeared *Maeve* was possibly guilty.

Maeve braced a hand on the back of a chair, breaking out in a sweat, her breathing quickening.

"Are you okay?" Nurse Biddy asked.

It was Garda Higgins all over again. When we'd feared the officer was having a heart attack after we'd confronted him about the whereabouts of Biddy's car, his guilt had caused a panic attack before he'd confessed.

Gretta and Biddy reached for Maeve, who held up a halting hand. She shrugged off her wool coat and accepted a glass of water from her mother. She appeared genuinely distressed. Yet she was obviously a skilled actress, having deceived Andrew, Gretta, and everyone in her life but her English relations and perhaps Andrew's adoptive parents.

I prayed Stella was behind the GenDNA scheme. There'd be no redeeming Maeve if she'd betrayed Andrew by monitoring his ancestry accounts to keep him from discovering his biological family. And had gone so far as to hire a bogus detective to scare off Gretta.

Maeve snatched her coat off the table. "I need to contact Andrew and warn him about this person. I just pray he believes me since he likely won't trust a word I say at this point."

"Hold off telling him," I said. "I think I know who's behind this." *If it's not you.* "Give me twenty-four hours to get the person to back off."

All eyes were on me. I refused to disclose Stella's identity. Gretta might run her second car off the road but on purpose this time.

"He might not *have* twenty-four hours," Maeve snapped.

"Then give me twelve. I wouldn't ask if I thought he was in serious danger in that time frame."

Maeve turned her stone-cold gaze on Gretta. "You had no right to take that test without asking for my blessing or at least telling me."

"You wouldn't have given me your blessing," Gretta said.

"Of course I wouldn't have! This all should have come from me. Not you. Doesn't matter now since Andrew wants nothing to do with either of us." Maeve gave Gretta a death glare, then spun around and stalked out of the pub.

Was that a *no* about her not warning Andrew and giving me time to get Stella to back off? If indeed Stella was to blame and not Maeve.

We all dropped down onto the benches, stunned, trying to process what had just happened. Now wasn't the time to blast Gretta for lying to me about telling Maeve she was searching for her son. Gretta stared into her empty tea mug, a lost look on her face. Rosie covered her mouth, stifling sobs. Biddy and I gulped down our waters, at a loss for words.

"Guess she won't be coming for New Year's," Gretta muttered.

I bit down on my lower lip to keep from bursting out laughing at Gretta's unintentional comedic timing. One of those awkward moments where you had a powerful urge to laugh uncontrollably to ease your stress.

"Appears she proved me wrong," Gretta said. "She *had* wanted to be a part of her son's life when I told her she'd only been wanting to keep the lad to spite me."

"Doesn't mean she'd have made a good mother," Biddy said.

I nodded. "If Bernie and Marion Marshall had somehow arranged the adoption and approved of the parents, they must be good people."

"I just hope he had a happy childhood. Guess I'll never know..."

"We most certainly will," Rosie said. "Once the lad calms down, he'll change his mind about meeting us. He may never have said he doesn't wish to see us. Maeve was merely saying that because she's upset."

"Oh, I'm sure she had a lot to say about me," Gretta said. "I can imagine the horrible things she told him, blaming me for giving him up for adoption."

"In all fairness to you," Rosie said, "Maeve made the final decision, not you. She could have gone against your wishes. And she certainly has a mind of her own, at least now."

"And Andrew can't blame *you* for her deceiving him his entire life," Biddy said.

"I bet he'll be open to meeting me," Rosie said. "And once I earn his trust, he'll be open to meeting you."

Gretta's gaze softened, and she gave Rosie's hand a squeeze. "Your Suzy Sunshine attitude used to drive me mad. But now I appreciate it." She pushed herself to her feet and headed out of the pub, too distraught to question me on who was behind the DNA plot.

"He'll come around," Rosie said. "I know he will. Why wouldn't he?" Tears filled the woman's eyes, betraying her optimistic tone.

Biddy and I assured her everything would be grand.

I placed a comforting hand on Rosie's arm. "Give him a bit to come to terms with it and see if he reaches out to us. If not, I'll get in touch with him."

Crap. I should have asked Maeve to confirm Andrew's last name. Not that she'd have shared it.

We walked toward the car, and Biddy and I trailed a distance behind the grandmothers.

"We have to take this to Garda Higgins," I said. "My gut tells me Stella's behind it. She likely has access to Sean's DNA account. She wanted revenge for her husband's affair. Wanted to keep Rosie from discovering her grandson and giving him the family estate. Stella undoubtedly assumed Rosie and Gretta would back off if they thought their grandson was a wanted criminal."

"She's a great actress, but is Maeve an even better one?"

I nodded reluctantly. "I know. Yet even though she managed to keep one of the biggest secrets ever from her son and parents for thirty-one years, like she said, Andrew was going to find out at some point. I seriously don't think she would have taken the risk of betraying his trust once again by planning such a devious scheme to keep him from discovering his biological family. That's more underhanded than not telling him she's his mother. She'd likely promised the adoptive parents she'd never disclose her identity. I could see Andrew forgiving her for the mom secret, but not if she'd been behind the criminal scheme."

Biddy shrugged. "I suppose."

"Besides, I've waited a year to see Stella behind bars. She's going down."

"If Stella is guilty, what was her plan in the end? Pay off Andrew to keep his mouth shut about his biological parents so she gets the full inheritance? Or not take a chance on his silence and silence him forever?"

"I'm afraid she'd be capable of it, but would she dare

since she knows we're onto her? She likely knows we don't have any real evidence. However, she doesn't know Garda Higgins owes us a favor."

I knew it wouldn't be long before we'd be calling in the favor. But had figured it would be more than seven weeks. Perhaps he wouldn't consider it the favor he owed us since arresting Stella was legally the right thing to do.

# Twelve

On the drive back from Dublin, everyone sat in silence. A George Michael marathon was playing on an eighties radio station. The song "Faith" came on, about a guy holding out hope for a better relationship and keeping the faith.

"Because I gotta have faith, faith..." I sang along under my breath, turning up the volume.

Biddy joined me in a hushed tone.

Even if Gretta and Rosie weren't familiar with the song, the perky tune and optimistic lyrics might lift their spirits. I peered in the rearview mirror at Rosie placing a comforting hand on Gretta's shoulder, giving her an encouraging look. The corner of Gretta's mouth twitched, but she was unable to manage a smile and went back to staring out the window.

We dropped off Gretta, then Rosie. Both women gave us a solemn goodbye without sticking around for words of encouragement. Besides singing the song lyrics, I didn't know if I had a pep talk in me. My positive attitude had diminished.

A half hour later, Biddy pulled into the Kilcarrigy Garda

station's lot and parked next to Garda Higgins's car. Thankfully, he was working. We entered the former cottage, where the officer sat at a wood desk surrounded by light-blue and gray walls. Recognition flickered in his blue eyes, and he gave us a pleasant yet apprehensive smile.

The white-bearded man's curious gaze narrowed on us. "Don't suppose you lasses are calling in to wish me a happy holiday?"

"Of course we be wishing you a happy holiday," Biddy said.

He arched a thick brow.

"Mightn't be our only reason for a visit though," she said.

We sat down in front of his desk. The man rubbed his beard while I recounted Stella's scheme and her plot to possibly harm Andrew.

"You need to arrest her before she heads to the Canary Islands for the holidays and never returns," I said.

Biddy nodded. "Probably has an offshore bank account filled with money."

He shook his head. "There's not enough evidence to be arresting her."

I let out a frustrated groan. "Not enough evidence? She has access to her husband's DNA account. She loses the—"

"Can you prove she has access to the account? Who says the fella hadn't deleted it before he died?"

"He died sooner than expected," I said. "I'm sure deleting his account was the last thing on his mind."

"Yet you don't see him as a match with this Andrew fella, his son?"

"Because she deactivated the account as soon as he showed up as a match with her husband," I said.

He shook his head again.

"When I mentioned Pringles, she became nervous," Biddy said.

Honestly, I'd become more nervous than Stella had.

The officer looked mildly intrigued. "What did she have to say about Pringles?"

Biddy's shoulders slumped. "She said the crisps were down the first aisle."

He let out a hearty laugh. "Serious, are ya?"

"Sean's will states that Stella receives the entire estate when Rosie dies *unless* there's an heir," I said. "That's motivation."

He shrugged. "Aye, it is. She has motive, I'll give ya that. It's the means and opportunity you need. Probable cause needs more than merely suspicion. Bring me solid evidence that she had access to the fella's DNA account along with her ability to have committed the crime. Doesn't seem plausible that she's flying over to Scotland each time she's emailing the lad."

"She's rerouting the IP address or has an accomplice," I said.

He gazed expectantly at me. "Who would that accomplice be?"

"Someone she knows." I dropped back against the chair in frustration, whereas Biddy perched on the edge of her chair, taking charge.

"How about ya go into the convenience store, buy some Pringles, and allude to the fact that ya know what she's up to? Touch on the key points of her scheme. *That* would be doing us a favor. We shouldn't be needing any evidence for that. Not like you'll be arresting her." Biddy gave him a definitive nod. "That'd be grand."

He rocked back in his chair, resting his hands on his belly. "Right, then. Because that whole Pringles crisp thing worked so well for you two?"

"We're not officers," Biddy said. "She'll take you more seriously."

"You *seriously* need more evidence and to work on a better scenario for opportunity. Then I'm happy to look into it. Not going to be losing my job by falsely accusing the woman and then having her file charges."

Biddy glared at the man. "Yeah, not everyone is as sympathetic and gracious as *I* am, not pressing charges."

"He's right." I pushed myself up from the chair. "We need more evidence to nail the woman."

"Would be grand if you could wait till after St. Stephen's Day. I spent last Christmas hunting down a thief robbing homes when people were at Mass. Would like to be enjoying this one."

"Yeah, I know," I said. "Thieves don't take holiday. Which reminds me. Have you had a thief swiping packages from porches?"

"We always have reports on packages being nicked from porches."

Biddy and I left the station feeling defeated.

"How are we going to get more bloody evidence on that wretched woman?" Biddy said.

"Opportunity is a biggie. We need to figure out if Stella was out of town when Noah received the emails."

"Right, then. No worries. We'll just drive over to her

store, threaten her with a can of Pringles, and demand to know if she happened to be in Scotland those dates."

I snapped my fingers. "I know. I'll send Ian the link to the store's website. Her photo is on it. Maybe he saw her skulking around there. Or what if Stella was the woman who'd offered to buy Ian a drink? Except he said she was gorgeous with auburn hair. Could have worn a wig, but no hiding her wrinkled tanned skin."

"But again, why would Stella have been in Holyhock?"

"Maybe she'd figured Andrew was a Pringle or worked for the company and went to their headquarters to snoop around for him. Same as Ian did. Then she had lunch at Mungo's, where she emailed Noah."

Fingers crossed that Ian could identify her. Proving Stella had the means to commit the crime was going to be a bit more difficult.

"Yet what if Stella is innocent and we're actually making her appear guilty, framing her?" Biddy said.

"We're not manufacturing evidence against her. Merely finding evidence already there to prove her guilt."

I prayed Stella was guilty, not Maeve.

On the drive home, I successfully avoided discussing Collin. I was a bit peeved he hadn't returned either of my messages. Biddy dropped me off, and I went straight for the mulled wine and peanut butter cookies. I'd been prepared for family drama when Gretta had spit her saliva into a tube nearly two months ago, but not to this extent. I took a gulp of wine, then settled in on the couch with my laptop to check my backup email address. No message from Andrew. I sank back against the couch and stuffed a cookie into my mouth. I pulled up Gretta's DNA account.

M.R. Pringle was gone.

No surprise he'd canceled or deactivated his account. Maeve certainly wouldn't have dared to do it.

If I were Andrew, I'd be questioning Maeve's intentions despite her denying her motivation for managing his account. She pretended to be helping him locate his biological family when actually she might have gone so far as concocting the GenDNA scheme to prevent him from learning the truth.

My phone rang on the table. Ian returning an earlier call. I explained my Stella theory and asked him to check out her photo on the store's website to see if he recalled her skulking around the area. It'd been easy enough for loser Noah to hop a flight to Edinburgh and take the train to Holyhock. Stella could have done the same. The mere thought of that woman caused heat to race up my neck to the tip of my ears.

"She's not the woman from the pub." Disappointment filled his voice. "Don't recall seeing her on the street or at the restaurant either. That tanned skin would have stood out among us pale Scots. Wouldn't have been wanting her to buy me a dram."

I heaved a frustrated sigh.

So much for opportunity, unless I could prove she'd rerouted the IP address.

I told him about our encounter with Maeve at the pub.

"Hadn't seen that one coming," Ian muttered. "Poor bloke. I suppose you and I were in a similar situation. Not that we'd had much contact over the years, but you believed I was your dad's second cousin rather than your father."

"In all fairness to *you*, you didn't know you were my father."

Silence filled the line.

This was the first time we'd discussed our relationship in depth since learning about it at the Clan Murray reunion. Amazingly, it didn't feel totally awkward. What happened to Andrew took betrayal to a whole other level than Ian and my situation. Mom likely hadn't known if Ian or Dad was my father. Not that it made what she did okay.

"The poor guy must be on a downward spiral," I said. "Feeling betrayed by his biological mother and his English relatives who likely knew Maeve's connection to him. Can't blame the adoptive parents, though, for making the choice not to tell him. And maybe Maeve had gone back on an agreement with them not to be in Andrew's life. She said when Andrew took the DNA test, he hadn't a clue he was adopted. He spent the past six months coming to terms with that, and now this happens. Once again turning his life upside down."

"You should reach out to the fella. Tell him you can relate to what he's going through. The shock of it anyway."

"I don't think he wants clichés right now. People telling him they know how he feels."

"Maybe *nobody* is telling him that because he has nobody to talk about it. He certainly can't turn to his family for comfort. Just see if he needs to talk."

After wishing Ian a safe flight in two days, I stared into the fire, thinking about his *fatherly* advice.

I phoned Dad for his opinion on whether I should reach out to Andrew.

"Do what your gut tells you to do," he said. "Not what

Ian or I say you should do. Only you know what's right for you."

"I'm just not sure if I should get further involved."

"Since when haven't you wanted to get involved when it comes to providing families with history, closure, or whatever they may need?"

"You're right."

"You don't need to ask my opinion because Ian gave you his and you agreed with him." He paused. "I'm sorry that Ian calling you his daughter threw me for a bit of a loop. It still takes some getting used to, but there's nobody else I'd rather share the title with."

My eyes watered. It wasn't just my family's situation. Everybody's family drama had me an emotional wreck right now.

"Okay, Mags?"

"Ah-hunh."

"Going to call Ian tomorrow to confirm our meeting location at the Dublin airport. Will see you in a few days."

I nodded, unable to squeak out goodbye without crying.

Ian was renting a car, saving Dad the stress of having to drive. They'd land within an hour of each other. Between the holiday traffic and tourists' first time driving in Ireland, I was happy to stay clear of the airport.

I wandered outside and inhaled several breaths of cool fresh air. Pinky cracked an eyelid from where he was napping on the front lawn. Five minutes of listening to my drama had the sheep snoozing away again. I went back inside and snuggled in the couch by the fire.

I pulled up Andrew's last email. I closed it, then opened a

new one, wanting us to have a fresh start. Not that he'd ever forget my involvement in ruining his life.

Fifteen minutes later, I tapped a finger against the computer keyboard, reading my email.

*How are you?*

Of course he was doing crappy. That was a ridiculous thing to ask. Yet what did I say to a guy whose last name I didn't even know. And he didn't know a thing about me. What he did know would likely cause him to block my email address. Telling him a bit about myself might make him more comfortable with me.

My genealogy website provided a detailed overview of me. The website's link autofilled in messages below my name on my regular email address but not on my backup one, so he hadn't seen it. Curious, he'd check out my website. What better way to share information about me? Perhaps too much about me?

The website promoted Dalwade Castle's cemetery project. Video clips from the two *Rags to Riches Roadshow* episodes. The tartan patterned dress I'd worn in the Halloween show and Dalwade Castle would give us a Scottish connection. Not to mention my last name, Murray, which he didn't even know. Even if he hadn't grown up in Scotland, he likely lived there now. I was also wearing Grandma's locket in that episode and talked about tracing Grandpa Fitzsimmons's ancestors, thanks to the heirloom that turned out to be a piece of mourning jewelry. Mourning jewelry, uncovering a skeleton, leading a cemetery restoration project, wanting to have met him at Glasnevin Cemetery...

If *I* didn't know me, I might think I was a tad creepy.

Still, I felt like I needed to give us some common ground

outside of the fact that I'd exposed the skeletons in his closet. I had to be up front about my connection to Gretta and not being some random genealogist. I refused to deceive him. Even if I sounded clichéd, at least I was being honest. And Ian was right. He might not have anyone else to turn to. I added a few lines telling him I'd experienced a similar situation to his, sort of, and I was here if he needed to talk. I added my website link and hit send.

My heart went berserk.

I was a genealogist who'd helped his grandmother hunt him down, forcing his mother to reveal a thirty-one-year-old secret and propelling his life into utter chaos.

*Stop overthinking it when the guy likely wouldn't even respond!*

But what if he did?

# Thirteen

I WOKE up to rain lightly tapping against my bedroom roof's window. Rain was relaxing when I was snuggled in bed or enjoying the ambiance in a cemetery. Not when I was caught in it while walking up to the pub or encountering cars on the narrow roads. The light ballet-slipper tapping grew into a loud rhythmic step-dancing number in a matter of seconds. I dragged myself out of bed, preparing to face the dreary day. Remembering my email to Andrew, I bolted down the spiral staircase to my laptop on the cocktail table. I checked my backup email address.

Nothing.

Had my website scared him off?

Was he put off by my cliché of knowing how he felt?

Or that thanks to me being a genealogist his life was a wreck?

The doorbell rang.

I ignored it, then decided it could be Gretta.

It was a delivery man with the package of monogrammed

golf balls. "Sorry about the delay. Have a happy Christmas." He turned to leave.

"Wait a sec. Where did this come from? I went to the house where it was misdelivered, and it wasn't there."

"Was in the home garage of another delivery driver." He gave me an apologetic shrug. "He's no longer with us."

"I would hope not. How did he think he could—" I snapped my mouth shut, not wanting to take my foul mood out on this poor guy. "Have a nice holiday." I went inside and set the box under the Christmas tree without opening it. At the moment, I couldn't have cared less about stupid golf balls.

I took a quick shower and dressed in jeans, a red sweater, and jingle bell earrings. Looking festive might help me get in the holiday spirit before Dad and Ian arrived tomorrow. Deciding Tommy and Gretta could also use some holiday spirit, I took a container of cookies and Norwegian pastries to the Lynches.

Fifteen minutes later Tommy and I were sitting across from each other in the yellow living room. He was dressed in flannel bottoms and a Jameson T-shirt. His bloodshot eyes stared at a peanut butter cookie before he devoured it in two bites, and then another.

"Hasn't come out of the bedroom since telling me about this bloody mess with Maeve." He shook his head. "Can't believe Maeve knew her son all these years without saying a word. Thought about ringing her but haven't a clue what to say. The poor lad must be a right mess."

Precisely why I'd reached out to him. Tommy might find a bit of comfort in the fact that I'd contacted Andrew to check on him. Yet if he didn't respond, Tommy and Gretta might lose hope of ever meeting their grandson.

George Michael's "Faith" played in my head.

I plucked the chocolate button off the top of a cookie and popped it into my mouth. Words of comfort seemed meaningless. I inhaled the rest of the cookie.

Tommy rubbed his stubbly chin. "I'd never have thought her capable of being so underhanded, claiming her son's a wanted criminal."

"In all fairness to Maeve, I don't believe she was behind that scheme. I think I know who was, and I'm trying to prove it."

A glint of hope flickered in his brown eyes. "Guess that would be something anyway."

Between the two of us, we polished off over a dozen cookies and pastries in under a half hour. Hopefully, Tommy had eaten the bulk of them. My jeans were already so tight I couldn't breathe. That or I was on the verge of a panic attack.

☘ ☘

Flour marred Rosie's flushed cheeks and the untied green apron hanging haphazardly over her wrinkled pink dress. Undoubtedly the first time the woman had ever pulled a dress from the dirty clothes hamper. No pearl necklace or makeup, and blue slippers covered her feet rather than proper heels. Rosie was a hot mess. She was baking like a madwoman to calm her nerves. It wasn't working.

Edmond shot me a worried look while preparing tea at the counter lined with an electric kettle, spice rack, standing mixer, and two cookie jars. He placed the steaming teacups on the kitchen table draped with a yellow-and-blue tablecloth and matching placemats. Very French provincial and cozy. Rosie added grated nutmeg in a mixing bowl and stirred the ingredients for Christmas pudding with fierce determination.

"Made pudding several weeks ago but thought another one might be a good idea." Rosie handed me the wooden spoon. "Need all the luck we can get right now."

I closed my eyes and slowly stirred the pudding clockwise, wishing for Andrew to respond to my email. The next stir was for the Lynches to put the pieces of their family back together. The last stir, to prove Stella guilty. Out of the three wishes, it was believed that one would be granted. Besides this tradition, it might be time to pay my fairy door a visit also.

I handed the spoon to Edmond, who made his three wishes.

"Poor Andrew," Rosie said. "He's the real victim in all of this. The lad just needs some time and he'll come around." Her eyes watered, and she braced a hand against the counter. "What if he doesn't? What if he never has the chance to know about his father or me?"

Edmond slipped an arm around Rosie's shoulders. "He'll be grand. 'Tis the season of perpetual hope."

"How am I going to break the news to the Bodkins after they made the decision to tell their family about Sean and to meet Andrew? And I feel for his adoptive parents. I hope he doesn't blame them. They might have had no choice but to agree to Maeve being in his life or she'd one day just shown up without their consent. That all might be forgivable, but Maeve possibly being the one to make us think he was a wanted criminal certainly isn't."

I shared my theory about Stella being behind the scheme.

Rosie's cheeks reddened. "That sounds just like her. Probably been monitoring Sean's DNA account since he passed away."

"Did he ever give you his account information? I could verify if it's still active and have Garda Higgins contact the company to confirm recent activity."

Rosie shook her head. "Sadly, I don't know a thing about his DNA accounts. He never mentioned canceling them anyway."

I told them about the sting operation. "There was a woman in the pub where Ian was that I hoped would turn out to be Stella, but it wasn't. I showed him the convenience store's website. He didn't recognize her from the pub or Mungo's."

Rosie's gaze narrowed. "Her best friend lives just south of Edinburgh. At least she used to. I think I have a snap of her from Sean and Stella's twentieth anniversary." Rosie went into the living room and returned with a photo album. She paged through it and pointed out a picture. "That's her."

A slim, pretty woman with the most gorgeous auburn hair I'd ever seen. Precisely how Ian had described the woman in the pub.

My heart raced. "I bet it's her. Can I take a shot of it?"

"You can have it, luv." Rosie slipped the photo from the plastic sleeve and handed it to me. "Haven't a clue why any snaps of that woman are still in the album. But I'm glad it was." She smiled anxiously.

I took a picture of the photo and texted it to Ian.

He responded almost immediately.

I smiled wider than the Grinch. "We've got a winner."

"Ah, that's brilliant." Edmond gave Rosie a celebratory kiss.

Rosie placed a hand to her chest. "Sean must be rolling over in his grave right now. But I'm so happy for Gretta. Maeve not having been involved in that wicked plan might make it easier for everyone to come to terms with the situation. To forgive Maeve. I just hope Andrew will want to see the land his father was raised on. Land that will now be his."

One wish down and two to go...

"Wonder if Noah's friend had the wrong location for the IP address or Stella's friend had switched locations, wanting a pint rather than a latte." Biddy studied Sean and Stella's anniversary photo while I drove us to see Noah. "That Sean was fierce gorgeous. If he was such a player, wonder if he also had something going on with Stella's friend. She's quite lovely. Haven't a clue what he saw in Stella. She's not pretty on the outside or inside."

"Good thing Ian is madly in love with Rhona, or he might have had a fling with that woman who was playing him all along."

"We need to find your dad a woman."

"He's only here a week. Besides, who do we know that'd make a good match for him?"

"Emily at work is absolutely lovely. She lost her husband a few months ago."

"Oh, that's sad. They'd have something in common, losing a spouse."

"No, lost as in can't find him. He went to pick up takeaway and never came home. Yet his clothes disappeared from the closet two weeks later. She lost her first husband also. Actually, he died under rather suspicious circumstances. Hmmm... Her being in the medical field kind of has me wondering if it was an accidental death. Maybe her second husband got to wondering also and that's why he left."

"I think she's out. What about your mom's friends?"

Biddy shook her head. "That's pathetic that we can't think of *one* person to set him up with. If we can come up with someone, maybe he'd fall in love and move to Ireland."

That'd be nice.

My phone rang.

Garda Higgins. I told him Ian had identified Stella's friend in the photo from the pub in Holyhock.

"He says we still need more proof," I told Biddy.

Biddy snatched the phone from my hand. "We're having to work awfully hard for this *favor* ya supposedly owe us. If we provide all the proof and you arrest her, you're merely doing your job. Not a favor. Ya see the difference, do ya?" A few moments later, Biddy disconnected the call.

"What did he say?"

"We need more evidence." She fumed. "What are we supposed to do? Fly over to Edinburgh and kidnap Stella's friend until she confesses?" Biddy snapped her fingers. "Ian could show up at her house with a bottle of wine and get her to talk. Maybe she'd seriously been into him and not merely eavesdropping for her own benefit."

I rolled my eyes. "You're right though, there's no way we're wasting this as the favor Garda Higgins owes us. Or he needs to step it up. He could contact GenDNA on behalf of law enforcement and have them look up Sean's account. Maybe Stella is using the same bogus email address for her contact with Noah as well as Sean's DNA account. Noah needs to give us the address. After he screwed up the sting operation, he owes us big time."

We pulled into the convenience store's lot and parked next to Noah's car. We marched inside, where he was standing by the latte machine, flirting with a blond girl. He spotted us, and panic flashed in his eyes. He dashed out the side door, and we chased after him.

"Stop!" I yelled.

He came to a halt and spun around, sweating, raking a hand through his dark hair. "The fella's dead, isn't he? I messed up and got him killed?" His gaze darted around. "I'll never get back into training!"

"Get a grip," Biddy said. "He's not dead."

Yet he hadn't responded to my email.

"Mags here figured out who's behind it all."

Hopefully.

"Jaysus, the way you came at me I thought for sure the bloody fella was dead."

"You still shouldn't have gone over to Scotland," I said. "But since you did, can you identify the woman in this photo?"

He glanced at Sean and Stella's anniversary picture with her friend. "Ah, yeah, my mum does her hair. Works out of the house, so seen her 'round a few times."

Biddy turned to me. "The woman flies in from Edinburgh to have her hair done?"

Noah's brow wrinkled in confusion. "Why would she be flying in when she lives in Drumcara?"

I pointed out Stella in the photo. "You mean *this* woman?"

He nodded. "The other one looks a bit familiar too." He tapped a finger against the photo. "Seen her recently."

"At the pub in Holyhock?" I asked.

He snapped his fingers. "That's it. Nice looking for an old lady."

"She's only like fifty," I said.

He shrugged, then his eyes widened. "The two of 'em were in on it together?"

"As you'd say, we're unable to *divulge* that information." Biddy gave him a snarky smile. "At least not until we talk to the garda. And ya better keep your gob shut and don't be getting involved."

Noah having identified Stella, and Ian identifying her friend from the pub, was more than enough evidence against Stella.

"What about my other three hundred euros?" he said.

"If we get it, ya promise to keep quiet?" Biddy said. "Can't even be telling your mum."

"As if I'd be telling my mum. She'd be raging that I impersonated a guard."

"And give me that email address you were using to communicate with the person who hired ya."

Sadly, it was a generic address without identifying info, but Garda Higgins might be able to get details on it even if Noah's hacker friend couldn't.

"I kind of fancy this whole investigative genealogy thing," he said. "Thinking if I don't get back into garda training, might go to school for it. Or maybe you could train me."

I shook my head. "Not a chance. Ireland offers degrees in

family history studies. Knowing how to conduct traditional research is as important as understanding DNA analysis."

"Might start by ordering a DNA test."

"Don't be coming to me for assistance when you get the results. And be prepared for the unknown."

"Like that Ian fella? Mentioned he's your biological father."

"What else did he say?" I demanded.

"That was it." He pressed his hands out in defense. "Nice fella. Didn't get back to his place until late, and he ordered Indian. Still has his turntable from university and a massive Queen collection. I was wrecked getting up at five a.m. for my flight after too many IPA beers."

I knew from the Murray reunion that Ian was a craft beer connoisseur. I made a mental note he liked Indian food and the classic rock group Queen.

Noah went back to work, and we promised he'd receive his money before New Year's.

"We certainly have enough proof for Garda Higgins between Noah identifying Stella and Ian recognizing her friend from the pub," Biddy said. "And when a woman gets her hair done, it's like an hour of nonstop chitchat. Noah's mum was probably venting about her son being kicked out of garda training and moving back home. Stella sucked the poor fella right into her scheme."

I called the officer and left a message. "He better not have us on ignore status." Garda Higgins was doing us a favor and making sure Stella backed off.

☘ ☘

Garda Higgins returned my call and reluctantly agreed to meet us in the parking lot across from Stella's convenience store. Upon reviewing the evidence, he confirmed that he had enough proof to bring Stella in for questioning.

Biddy and I did a high five.

"I'm thinking maybe Stella used the Holyhock IP address so if the police ever discovered what she was doing, they'd figure it was someone at Pringle and Company involved."

He nodded. "You realize this could end up getting that Noah fella in trouble for impersonating an officer?"

"Can't we keep his name out of it?" I said.

"I'm guessing she'll give him up. Can't prove her motive was to prevent the lad from receiving the inheritance. She could claim she was searching for her late husband's son to ensure he received the land that was rightfully his."

"By invading Gretta's privacy under false pretenses?" I said. "Why would Stella have gone to such great lengths claiming he was a criminal except to get Gretta and Rosie to back off? How's that not illegal?" I curled my fingers into fists.

He gave me a sympathetic look. "The woman is a dodgy creature altogether. I agree. But it could be quite the process to get a conviction of any sort. Do ya think the family wants to be dealing with all the drama? Sounds like they have plenty as it is."

My shoulders slumped. "You might be right."

Biddy smacked my arm. "Mad, are ya? After you've been going on about wanting the woman to be guilty, you're going to let her get off? And what about the fact that she knows we're onto her? What if she runs us off the road?"

"If ye be showing up dead, I'll know who's to blame." The officer smiled at Biddy.

She tossed her arms up in frustration. "Ah, that's grand, isn't it now?"

"Only messing with ya," he said.

"He's right," I said. "I wasn't thinking rationally about putting Andrew through even more drama trying to prove Stella intended to harm him. Our main concern right now should be getting the woman to back off and hopefully move to the Canary Islands."

Biddy let out a defeated huff. "This should only count as half a favor," she told the officer. "We did all the work."

"I'm paying for the crisps," he said.

Garda Higgins entered the convenience store. He gave Stella a nod hello and headed straight for the snack aisle. Biddy and I waltzed inside, ignoring Stella's glare. We perused the beverage cooler across from her.

The guard set two canisters of Pringles on the counter. "My favorite crisps. Have a friend, Andrew, over in Scotland who I believe works for Pringle and Company."

Stella slid us a discreet yet panicked gaze.

"A woolen goods company out of Holyhock," the officer said. "I guess they have lovely goods. Ever heard of 'em?"

Stella nodded faintly, handing him his change.

"I really should be paying my friend, Andrew, a visit one day soon." He grabbed his crisps and gave Biddy and me a wink on his way out.

We were on.

"Seems the garda officer isn't the only one with a friend in Scotland." I slapped Stella's anniversary photo on the counter. "Someone spotted your friend at Mungo's restaurant in Holyhock a few days ago."

"Familiar with the restaurant, are ya?" Biddy demanded.

Stella's breathing quickened.

"You owe Noah Kenny three hundred euros," I said.

"Might want to make that five hundred considering the risk he took impersonating an officer," Biddy said.

Stella's jaw tightened.

Hush money. We were no better than Cousin Millie!

Biddy stuck her nose in the air. "And ya owe us a box of chocolates."

"You may want to sell your business and retire to the Canary Islands sooner than planned," I said. "Just a thought."

I called Gretta and gave her the skinny on Stella so she could assure Maeve that her son was no longer in danger. Hopefully, Stella's place was on the market and the woman was gone before we decorated the gingerbread castle for the New Year's auction.

☘   ☘

That evening I was dusting the living room while watching *Frosty the Snowman*, struggling to stay away from the mulled wine and cookies. An arriving email dinged on my laptop.

Andrew.

Heart racing, I sat on the edge of the couch cushion with my computer and read the message.

*Thanks for the email. Your ghost hunter video was brilliant. Seen the fellas' videos before. Loved the tartan dress in the Halloween episode. Didn't realize I was talking with a celebrity and ghost hunter.*

I laughed. If I ever did encounter a ghost, with my luck, it'd be hunting me rather than me hunting it.

*Finding a skeleton was a bit mad, and solving a cold case.*

He'd apparently clicked through from the ghost hunters video clip to the viral Twitter post that had landed us the gig. The pic of Biddy and me covered in mud, which led people to believe the photo was taken while we were digging up the skeleton, not the day after our find.

Maybe I hadn't heard from him earlier because he'd been busy reading up on me. Hmm...

*You're brilliant at business promo.*

It was more like dumb luck.

*I'm in market research.*

I didn't wish to be a case study.

If I wasn't already.

I didn't want to play dumb and ask what products he researched. However, I didn't know for sure that he worked for Pringle's even though M.R. likely stood for market research. So I asked.

*Work for a woolen goods company where my father worked. Based in Glasgow. Live a half hour north. A five-minute walk to the local pub. What more could a fella want?*

Exactly! I told him about my hangout at Biddy's family pub, McCarthy's.

My fingers were flying across the keyboard, shooting emails back and forth. A glass of wine and several cookies later, we were on the topic of my numerous seasonal jobs. From my first one at age nineteen harvesting cranberries in Oregon to being a banquet server on an Alaskan cruise ship.

He laughed at the story about a rogue flame from a baked Alaska once singing off my eyebrow, a sliver of which never grew back.

In college he'd been a professional queuer, standing in line for people who had more money than time. Like for the latest hot tech device or concert tickets. He'd camped out for two days once for Rolling Stones tickets and was paid twenty pounds an hour. He'd also been a golf ball diver for several resorts outside Edinburgh. His job was fishing out the stray balls golfers hit into ponds.

I told him my dads loved golf and would get a kick out of that story. And about the misdelivered golf ball debacle. Also, that speaking of Edinburgh, my biological father lived there.

When he didn't respond, my body kicked into panic mode.

What if he thought I was trying to segue into a conversation about why I had two dads and had mentioned I'd experienced a similar situation to his?

Radio silence.

Should I dampen the conversation by asking how he was doing with everything that happened? If he had a desire to meet Gretta or Rosie? A conversation we were both avoiding. Several minutes ticked by. I finally asked if he was still there.

*Yep, but gotta go. Cheers*

I told him thanks for chatting.

I flopped back onto the couch in frustration.

Hopefully, for Rosie and Gretta's sake, I hadn't scared him off. And for mine. Not only did I want to help him out, but I couldn't recall the last time I'd had so much fun chatting with a guy. A guy I'd never even met. Fingers crossed I hadn't blown my chance at meeting him.

# Fourteen

IF IT WEREN'T for Dad and Ian arriving early that afternoon, I'd have stayed in bed the following day. Not only was I depressed over Andrew having abruptly ended our email conversation after I'd mentioned my biological father in Edinburgh, but a year ago today had kicked off Grandma's two-day wake. Double whammy. And I was worried about Gretta and Rosie. To think, a week ago I'd been nervous about spending the holidays with Dad and Ian. Now that was the least of my worries.

Skipping a shower, I threw on my cleaning clothes from the hamper—worn jeans and a stained white T-shirt that reeked of bleach. I schlepped the vacuum cleaner up the spiral staircase. Lying on the wood floor, I swept the long tube under my bed, sucking up dust bunnies, dead flies, and an earring I'd been missing for five years. The fact that Grandma and I both despised cleaning made me smile.

The doorbell rang.

Startled, I bumped my head against the wooden frame. I pushed myself out from under the bed, blowing at a dust bunny hanging from my eyebrow. Heading down the stairs, I spied a moving truck parked in front of my fence. Lost delivery drivers asking for directions wasn't uncommon. However, I peered out the window at the best-dressed delivery man I'd ever seen. A gorgeous dark-haired guy in a tan wool peacoat and jeans. The last time a cute guy had stood at my door, I'd been duped. Still, I darted from view and swept a hand over the top of my head to brush away any cobwebs. I opened the door.

The guy gave me a hesitant smile. "Mags?"

"Ah, yeah, can I help you?"

"I'm Andrew."

My breathing quickened.

As in Gretta's and Rosie's grandson Andrew?

"Andrew the line queuer and golf ball diver?" I asked.

He nodded, raising the red gift bag in his hand. "Brought golf balls to prove it. Hit into the pond by famous golfers and celebrities and fished out by me." He handed me the bag. "I identified each ball. I was friends with the manager of one resort. He always had me clean out a pond before a pro or celebrity match. That way I could track golfers' balls. I kept Billy Casper's, though, from when he visited the resort. One of my favorite golfers."

Casper. Andrew's GenDNA profile name.

"Wow, that's a way better gift than monogrammed golf balls." One of the sweetest things a guy had ever done for me. I peered into his dreamy brown eyes with thick dark lashes, losing my train of thought. "Um, thanks. That was nice of you to deliver them in person."

"Ah, I hope me being here is okay." He shifted his stance. "I should have rang before hopping a plane. After our emailing last night, I stayed up trying to decide what to do about my wreck of a life. Next thing I knew, I was at Glasgow airport. Surprised I could get a ticket." He gestured to the delivery truck. "No car hires available though. Was lucky to get the lorry." He blinked back raindrops starting to fall. He had Sean's brown eyes, based on the photos I'd seen.

"I'm sorry. Come in." I stepped aside, a nervous fluttering in my stomach.

He entered the mudroom along with a fresh woodsy scent that I hoped camouflaged my eau de bleach smell. His gaze narrowed on my missing sliver of eyebrow, and he reached a hand toward my face. My heart raced with anticipation. He plucked a dead fly from the top of my head and flicked it outside.

I swallowed the nervous lump in my throat. "Thanks. Was cleaning."

He stepped into the living room. "This is the most spontaneous thing I've ever done. I'm not the adventurous type, unlike you."

"I don't look for adventure. It just seems to find me."

We shared a laugh, easing the nervous tension.

He shrugged off his wool jacket and draped it over the back of the couch while I placed the red gift bag under the tree next to the box of monogrammed golf balls. I went into the kitchen for beverages and peeked at my reflection in the glass covering a picture on the wall. I finger-combed my messy hair and grabbed a chip-clip from a bag of Taytos and tossed my hair up on my head. I snatched a linen-scented dryer sheet from under the sink and swept it over my cleaning clothes. Thankfully, Grandma's spices remained in the rack. Not having brushed my teeth, I took a swig of peppermint extract, setting my mouth on fire. I returned to the living room with two bottled waters and a plate of Biddy's and my frosted cookies. I sat on the love seat across from Andrew on the couch.

"You're probably wondering how I found you," he said.

"My website says I live in a former schoolhouse in the Midlands. I'd mentioned the pub up the road, so you searched out McCarthy's pubs in central Ireland, and the plaque on my house says Ballycaffey National School."

An intrigued smile quirked the corners of his mouth.

We had supersleuthing skills in common.

That quality was even more attractive than his looks. After my twenty-four-hour engagement to Josh and a short-lived relationship with Finn, I swore I'd never make the mistake of falling for a guy because of his looks. However, I already liked Andrew because of his wit, and he was easy to talk to.

Not that I was *falling* for Andrew.

"Sorry about going MIA on you last night," he said. "Tell me about your dad in Edinburgh."

I recounted the story of a DNA test's life-altering news that my biological father was Dad's second cousin.

"Wow. Same way I discovered my adoption. Through a DNA test. After the shock wore off, at least a bit, I confronted my adoptive parents, who had no choice but to tell me the truth. DNA doesn't lie. But they never disclosed Maeve's my mother."

"I couldn't confront my mom. She died a year before I took the test."

Andrew frowned. "I'm sorry." Compassion filled his brown eyes, urging me to open up.

"Lately I've been thinking it might be better that I didn't have the chance to ask her about it. It wouldn't have changed what happened. If I'd taken the test a year before her death, we'd possibly have been estranged at the time she'd died. I'd never have gotten over the regret of not being around her final year. And it would have hurt my dad in the end."

Honestly, that thought had just popped into my head. It was the most rational one I'd had about Mom since learning Ian was my father.

Andrew nodded, a pensive look on his face. "Not sure what will happen between me and Maeve. Who knows if she'd have told me the truth if she hadn't been forced to?"

"Honestly, I think she planned to tell you. Gretta showing up as your match threw her for a loop, and she panicked. Wasn't able to think straight." I shrugged. "I don't know. It's a complicated situation."

"Always called her Auntie Maeve because I had no aunts, or uncles for that matter." He peered over at the tree in the corner. "She never forgot a birthday or Christmas."

I nodded. "Ian and his brothers visited when I was seven. Brought me a Lady Mags Murray T-shirt from Scotland. Two months ago he gave me a ten-foot-by-ten-foot plot of land in the Highlands. Now I'll forever have the Lady Mags Murray title even though the T-shirt no longer fits."

Andrew laughed, relaxing back against the couch.

The doorbell rang.

His smile vanished, and our panicked gazes locked.

What if it was Gretta?

My heart went berserk as I walked out to the mudroom, where Biddy was peeking through the door's window. I let out a relieved whoosh of air.

I opened the door a crack. "Come back later."

"A fella just came into the pub and said there's a moving truck at your house. I came straight away to make sure some dodgy fellas hadn't broken in and were cleaning out the place."

"I'm fine. Come back in a bit."

"Why's that lorry..." Fear flashed in Biddy's eyes. She placed a finger to her temple, mimicking a gun.

"Promise I'm not holding her at gunpoint," Andrew said behind me. "You're Biddy. Recognize you from Mags's videos on her website."

I introduced them and reluctantly allowed Biddy inside.

Biddy's gaze narrowed on Andrew. "Janey, you look like Sean." She turned to me. "Doesn't he be looking like Sean?"

"Sean was your father," I told him, unsure if Maeve had shared his father's name or identity.

"Never gave Maeve a chance to tell me about him," he said. "I was raging and cut her off."

"It's not our place to tell you anything more about your family," I said. "It's your grandmothers'. Gretta and Rosie live right up the road. Can I give them a call?"

I hadn't told either woman that I'd contacted Andrew. They'd be surprised yet happy about the outcome.

Andrew nodded with hesitation.

My stomach tossed in anticipation as I slipped my phone from my back pocket. With any luck, everyone's lives would be changing for the better this time.

Fifteen minutes later Edmond and Rosie stood on my front stoop, wearing anxious smiles. Gretta looked pale, on the verge of fainting.

"I can't believe he's here," Rosie whispered, peering past me and into the mudroom. "Making those wishes worked." The Christmas pudding I'd stirred while making three wishes sat on a white china plate in Rosie's hands.

Edmond held a large photo album, and Gretta held her breath as they entered the house. Andrew stood in the living room, peering nervously at his grandmothers.

Rosie gasped in surprise, releasing her hold on the china plate. Edmond swooped in with the photo album, catching the plated dessert halfway to the floor.

Unfazed by Edmond's heroic feat, Rosie continued staring at Andrew. "It's as if Sean is standing before me." She placed trembling fingers against her lips. "Certainly don't be needing a DNA test to tell me you're my grandson."

Gretta shook her head, remaining speechless.

I gave Andrew an encouraging nod, and he smiled at Rosie. "So I've heard."

"That's *all* he's heard," Biddy said. "We were leaving the family information for you ladies to share."

"Even your build reminds me of Sean..." Rosie's gaze swept up and down the length of her grandson several times.

Tall, broad shoulders, and a trim physique, Andrew looked like he enjoyed hiking in the Scottish Highlands and kayaking around the Isle of Skye or the Outer Hebrides. I'd always wanted to try kayaking. Perhaps he'd be interested in taking me around a small loch to get my feet wet.

"Of course, you look like a Bodkin, seeing as Sean was adopted." Rosie smiled. "Oh, you'll adore the Bodkins. Such a lovely couple. Maybe I should give them a ring and invite them over."

Apprehension flickered in his eyes.

Edmond placed a hand on Rosie's arm. "It's probably best to be holding off on too many introductions in one day."

Rosie nodded. "Of course. But I must introduce you to your father." She hurried over to the couch and patted the cushion next to her. "Come. I'll show you his snaps."

Andrew sat on one side of her, Edmond on the other. Biddy and I relaxed back on the love seat, while Gretta squeezed between us and perched on the edge of the cushion.

Rosie placed the photo album on her lap and pointed out a picture on the first page. "He'd have been merely five years younger than you in this one when he received his pilot's license." She smiled proudly.

Andrew's gaze narrowed on the photo. "He looks familiar."

"Indeed," Rosie said. "Looks just like you, he does."

He shook his head. "No, I know him. Or rather *knew* him." A look of shocked disbelief washed over him. "Died five years ago, didn't he?"

Rosie and Gretta shared confused glances.

"How did you know that?" Rosie asked.

He peered up at her then over at Gretta. "He was Maeve's boyfriend."

Gretta's eyes widened. "Maeve's boyfriend?"

"She was heartbroken when he passed away. I'd gone to see her, worried. They'd been together for years. Was surprised they'd never married."

"Because he was already married." She frowned, placing a

hand to her chest. "Can't believe Sean never told me about you."

"Can't believe neither of them told *me* any of this." Andrew's cheeks reddened over one more betrayal.

"You're right, luv." Rosie placed a hand on Andrew's, and he relaxed slightly. "This must be much more difficult for you than any of us. Yet I'm happy you had the chance to know Sean." A tear trailed down Rosie's cheek. "Please don't think badly of him for being with Maeve when he was married. Stella's not a good person. If it'd been easier to do so in Ireland, I'm sure they'd have divorced years ago."

Stella had possibly known about Sean and Maeve's affair and their son. She'd have wanted him to remain a secret as much as they had.

"Did you know Sean well?" Edmond asked Andrew.

Andrew nodded faintly, pressing his hands on the top of his legs, appearing to gather his thoughts. "Met him when I was ten. He came to a soccer match when my team was in the finals. Was also at my university graduation. Saw him a dozen times or so over the years. Yet never had a clue he was my father. Never noticed the resemblance. Never dreamed..." He choked back his emotions, closing his eyes.

"Take your time, dear," Gretta said, wiping a tear from her cheek.

"That's right." Rosie gave his leg a pat. "Plenty of time to discuss everything. Like if you'll be wanting the family land and home Sean grew up in. Not that you have to live there, but it'll be yours to do with as you please. That's what Sean wanted. And it appears he knew what he was doing when he put an heir in his will."

I wasn't going to make this visit more difficult or

awkward by telling Andrew about Stella and her GenDNA scheme. I'd save that for after his grandmothers left. If Maeve had called him about it in a panic, I think he'd have mentioned it.

"It's just a few miles up the road," Rosie said.

"Walking distance to McCarthy's pub?" Andrew asked me.

I nodded. "In the opposite direction of the pub."

He smiled, sending a flush of heat through my entire body.

"Every place in a five-mile radius is walking distance to our pub," Biddy said. "You'll have to try our famous pizza."

Gretta cupped a hand over her mouth, catching a sob. I slipped an arm around her shoulders.

Andrew's gaze softened on his grandmother. "She truly loved him."

Gretta wiped away tears, clearing her throat. "And I kept them apart."

"Don't be ridiculous," Rosie snapped. "He was married. You did what you thought was best for Maeve and Andrew."

Gretta nodded faintly. "I'm sure Maeve told you I was responsible for her putting you up for adoption."

He shook his head. "She didn't."

Gretta appeared surprised.

"It's only natural for a mother to want her young unwed daughter to put her child up for adoption for everyone's best interest," Rosie said.

"My parents...my adopted parents are brilliant. I had a great childhood." Andrew took a deep breath. "When I discovered I was adopted, some pretty bad scenarios went through my head. I never imagined this one. Yet it's better than some others." He smiled at Gretta, who relaxed back against the couch.

"Well, I certainly need to be apologizing for my cousin Millie out in Galway, claiming you're her nephew. The woman hasn't a clue. Hadn't seen her for thirty years and don't plan to for another thirty. Will be ringing her though, telling her I've met my grandson and she won't be getting a cent out of me. She's the worst apple in the bunch. You'll get on grand with your uncles and of course your grandfather, Tommy. He was out when Mags called about you being here." Gretta wiped a tear from her cheek. "Sorry. I'm a wreck."

"How about some Christmas pudding?" Rosie said, lightening the mood.

Everyone agreed that was a great idea and chatted while Rosie and I plated slices of pudding—a dome-shaped sticky cake made with dried fruit and spices. We returned to the living room and distributed the dessert and tea. I bit into something hard and slipped it from my mouth. A small silver ring. Grandma hadn't followed the tradition of hiding coins and charms in Christmas pudding. I'd have preferred a Christmas coin, which was believed to bring good luck and wealth.

"Oh my, you got the ring," Rosie said.

Edmond gave me a sly smile. "Means you'll be married within the coming year."

It would have been more appropriate for Rosie to have gotten the ring since Edmond was proposing on Christmas Eve.

"Married within a year," Biddy mused, shooting Andrew a discreet glance.

Thankfully, he was occupied with his dessert and missed Biddy's bold comment.

I laughed it off. "I believe a silver ring or crown can mean the person has to be treated like a king or queen for the night. And it brings good fortune the following year." I peered around at my guests. "I'm already feeling quite fortunate. However, I don't mind being promoted from *Lady* Mags Murray to *Queen* Mags."

Andrew quirked an intrigued brow. "And you have Dalwade Castle to go with your title."

I smiled, nodding. Since several of my family members had invested in the hotel, I might one day inherit part of the medieval castle. Yet nothing could ever be better than owning Grandma's cozy Irish cottage filled with wonderful memories and a promising future.

## Fifteen

THE FOLLOWING NIGHT, Christmas Eve, I opened my front door to find Biddy wearing a red *Feliz Navidad* T-shirt.

"*Bon soir* and *Feliz Navidad*!" She gave me a big hug. "I know *Feliz Navidad* is Spanish. It was the closest thing to French that Collin could find. I haven't had time to look through my French phrase book for how to say it. Came here straight away. I'm going to Paris!"

Phew. The Paris trip was on. Must have been my threatening voicemail about Biddy and me going to Paris to find French guys that made Collin get it together. Good thing Biddy had changed her mind and given Collin a romantic weekend getaway to the castle hotel instead of cookie ornaments.

Biddy let out an excited squeal and flew past me. Inside Dad and Ian were relaxing in the living room with a craft beer I'd picked up. "I'm going to Paris!"

She slipped her arms around Dad's shoulders from behind the couch and gave him a hug. The green tissue-paper crown flew from the top of his slightly graying dark hair.

Discarded cardboard tubes from the traditional Christmas crackers littered the rug. Plastic trinkets, slips of papers with jokes, and other prizes were scattered across the cocktail table. Dad was a good sport, wearing the crown and the reindeer tie I'd bought him years ago.

"Have a chocolate crepe for me," Dad said. "Lived on them the time I went to Paris for work." A sparkle twinkled in his blue eyes.

Ian and Dad had the same bright-blue eyes that made them look more like brothers than second cousins, sharing great-grandparents rather than parents.

"That'll be great craic." Ian stood and gave Biddy a congratulatory hug, rattling off something in French.

Biddy's jaw dropped, and she stared at him in awe. "Guess I won't be needing a phrase book, seeing as I have a private tutor."

Dad gave Ian a pat on the back. "You walked right into that one, buddy."

"Aye. That I did." Ian laughed.

"*Mais oui.*" Biddy smiled proudly. "I'll be a totally brill student. I'm already mastering the language. We're going to the top of the Eiffel Tower, where Collin is *not* proposing." She shot me a knowing look.

"I didn't tell him *not* to propose. Just asked if he *was* proposing. The guy was a nervous wreck about the trip being perfect."

"Are ya completely mad? Neither of us is ready for marriage." She peered over at Dad and Ian. "Mags got me a lovely designer blouse that is très chic. Perfect for the trip."

It was très Mark and Spencer.

"I just wanted to pop over and share the news and give

you this." Biddy handed me a small box wrapped in colorful snowmen paper. "The pub is closed. We're getting ready for a wicked game of 30 Seconds. Happy Christmas," she yelled over her shoulder as she breezed out the door.

"Watch out, Paris," Dad said.

We all laughed.

"Sorry, but you won't find a trip to Paris in my gift," Ian said.

"Think you'll like ours even better than Paris." Dad wore a mysterious grin.

"Wow, I'm intrigued. Paris is stiff competition."

We cleaned up so we'd have a place to open the gifts. The cardboard scraps of party favors filled a garbage bag. Christmas crackers were a great icebreaker. I'd stocked up on two dozen just in case there was any awkwardness between us three spending our first holiday together. There wasn't. Since Dad and Ian had arrived yesterday, we'd been hanging out at McCarthy's pub and visited Rosie, Edmond, and the Lynches. They'd met Andrew briefly before he headed to the airport. Besides not having packed a suitcase, Andrew wanted to spend the holiday with his parents, the Buchanans. A very regal surname. He was returning to Ireland for St. Stephen's Day and to help decorate the ginger-bread castle. Suddenly, I was looking forward to decorating gingerbread.

"Open this one first." Dad handed me a small box wrapped in red sparkly paper. "It's from us both."

I tore off the paper and removed the top off a fancy aqua-colored box. It contained a round silver ornament decorated with the Murray blue, green, and red plaid tartan. Engraved in the center was *Lady Mags Murray, 1995*. The letters curved along the top read *Ryan Murray*, the bottom *Ian Murray*.

A lump of emotion lodged in my throat, and tears filled my eyes. Dad and Ian embraced me in a group hug.

"It's perfect," I muttered.

Next I opened Ian's gift, which included three ornaments. A vintage blown-glass one of Santa dressed in full Scottish kilt attire playing a bagpipe. A cardboard cutout sheep, its wool made with cotton balls, yellowed from the years. And a stuffed sheep wearing a blue-and-green kilt.

"As a lad, first thing I did when I arrived at my Murray grandparents' was to march around the house with the Santa ornament playing an imaginary bagpipe. Was mad into bagpipes. My grandparents gave me lessons one year for Christmas. Took a few and quit. Turned out my lungs weren't as strong as everyone thought."

We all laughed.

"Bet you can't guess which sheep I made when I was ten and which is a new addition to our family ornaments."

I held up the cotton-ball sheep with a red ribbon strung through a hole in the top.

"Aye. Can't believe you had it right." Ian smiled, a dimple creasing his cheek.

I admired the ornaments. "These are precious."

Dad's gift box contained three familiar ornaments. One of my grandma Murray's delicate crocheted snowflakes. A tiny green-and-red winter cap Mom had knitted. A hobby she'd given up after cussing the entire time while making the ornaments. And a snowman I'd made from bread dough in art class.

"Appears I wasn't talented enough to make ornaments

when I was a boy, so thought I'd give you one of yours," Dad said.

"You guys were right. These are way better than a trip to Paris. But don't tell Biddy that. I'm guessing it's thanks to her I have all these wonderful family memories?"

Dad nodded. "But we selected them."

I held out a heavy box. "This idea was Andrew's and mine. It's for both of you."

Ian quirked a brow. "Already giving gifts as a couple, are ya?"

"Ha-ha. Open it."

The box contained twenty golf balls in plastic baggies with the golfer or celebrity name written in marker on each. I'd also printed off a photo of the display case I'd ordered for both of them and would be labeling with the golfers' names. I explained Andrew's previous job as a golf ball diver.

"To be fair, and not cause any fights on Christmas Eve, you each get to select one ball at a time," I said.

Dad's first choice was Bill Murray.

"I knew you'd choose that one." I peered over at Ian. "He has watched *Caddyshack* like a hundred times."

"Don't forget *Scrooged*."

"Maybe we're related to the bloke," Ian said.

"Never thought of that." Dad turned to me.

"Yeah, I'm right on top of that. I'll find our Murray connection in all my spare time."

Ian chose Halle Barry's ball. "Brilliant actress."

I smiled. "Yeah. I'm sure it's merely her acting abilities you're attracted to. What about Tiger Woods and Phil Mickelson?"

Ian shrugged. "Those are great. Yet I wouldn't be able to find a ball hit by Halle Barry on eBay."

Professional golfers were the last ones chosen.

Dad selected the movie stars while Ian chose the only two rock stars, Alice Cooper and Bob Seger. I was learning more and more about Ian.

I shook Biddy's gift. "Gee, do you think this might be— an ornament?" I opened the box to find a crystal ornament displaying a photo of Biddy and I wearing elf hats. My first Christmas with Grandma when I was twelve. I was tearing up until I removed the tissue paper from the plastic ornament with Birdie in a colorful Christmas sweater. I burst out laughing.

Dad eyed Birdie's photo. "A friend of yours?"

"A relation of Gretta's."

"She mightn't want to be telling Andrew about that one," Ian said.

"I doubt he'll ever meet Birdie or Cousin Millie."

I added the new ornaments to the tree and admired them through a blurry-eyed haze. "This is by far the best family tree I've ever created. Thanks to the help from the best friends and family ever."

We clinked our drink glasses and toasted our first Christmas together. "*Sláinte.*"

And to many more ornaments in my future.

# Sixteen

FOUR DAYS LATER

"I lost my ring!" Rosie's hand shot up in the air, her pearl engagement ring missing. "It must have happened when I changed my plastic gloves." Her gaze darted from the bucket filled with white frosting to the three-foot-high gingerbread replica of Malahide Castle.

Dad snapped back the spatula in his hand for spreading frosting on the castle's roof. Ian, Collin, and Biddy did the same. Andrew and I froze, each of us holding a peppermint candy in midair for decorating the last turret.

Rosie and Edmond had been filling and distributing the plastic frosting bags with a one-inch opening on the end. The ring could be anywhere!

"We have to find it!" Rosie snatched the spatula from Biddy's hand, preparing to scrape away the frosting.

"Don't be damaging it!" Gretta sprang from the chair

where she and Tommy were sitting at a table, placing green leaf-shaped gummies on cardboard cutouts of shrubs and ivy vines.

Everyone searched the castle's exterior.

I dropped to my knees and scanned the front, decorated with red and green gumdrops and gumballs.

A glint of silver caught my eye in the white frosting trimming the door. "I think I found it!" Using the tip of a knife, I plucked the ring from the frosting.

Relieved sighs filled the air.

Rosie gave me a huge hug, then cleaned off the ring with a napkin and polished it. She tucked it safely inside her wallet. "I won't be removing the ring until I arrive at the jewelers to have it properly sized. And then Edmond can keep it until our wedding in March." Rosie gazed lovingly at her fiancé.

The couple was getting married at Dalwade Castle. I was their maid of honor, and Andrew was the best man. The thought of him in a dark suit and tie took my breath away. Archie gave us a great deal for nearly buying out the place. Photos of the celebration would make a wonderful addition to the hotel's website.

"That's the second ring you've found within a week," Gretta mused with interest. "Including the one in the Christmas pudding."

Biddy gave me a sly grin. "It is, isn't it now?"

A curious glint flickered in Andrew's brown eyes, causing a warm sensation to rush up my neck and across my cheeks.

When I'd ended my relationship with Finn, I'd promised

myself I'd find a man with four qualities Finn hadn't possessed.

Number one—someone I wanted to spend time with as much as I did Biddy. Check. The past week I'd been spending more time with Andrew than Biddy. Partly because she and Collin were planning their Paris trip. I'd given Andrew a grounds tour of Kiernan Moffat's estate, where Biddy and I'd uncovered the skeleton and filmed my second episode on *Rags to Riches Roadshow*. Then the cemetery where I'd discovered the dead body on my grandparents' graves. And of course McCarthy's pub. Andrew got a kick out of the photo of me on the pub's wall after a sheep had chased me up the road and inside the place.

Number two—someone who was as passionate about genealogy as I was. Check. Nobody would ever be *as* passionate about ancestry research, but Andrew enjoyed listening to my stories and understood my obsession. He'd offered to assist me in researching Gretta's maternal family tree. Hopefully, I didn't discover any relation worse than Cousin Millie.

Number three—someone who lived within an hour drive from me. He didn't *live* at Rosie's, but he'd been staying with his grandmother. If Rosie's house didn't one day become his permanent home, it would at least be a vacation home.

Number four—someone who didn't eat lamb. I wasn't sure if he liked the meat or not. However, that one wouldn't be a deal breaker. Besides, he'd already grown quite fond of Pinky. Using Froot Loops as an incentive, Andrew had trained the sheep to do circles around the rose trellis and kiss my cheek. A year ago I'd never dreamed I'd be letting a sheep get close enough to kiss me.

Andrew, Pinky, and I were off to a great start.

The pastry chef had left us in a room off his shop while he prepared orders for New Year's Eve events. We took a break to recover from the missing ring debacle. Dad and Ian chatted with Andrew about their spring golf outing.

"You should join us," Dad told Andrew. "It's the least we can do. Thanks to you I have a golf ball hit into a pond by my favorite actor, Bill Murray."

"Think I'll put Halle Barry's on my desk," Ian said.

"I'd fancy joining you," Andrew said. "Just to warn you, though, I won't be diving for your golf balls."

"No worries." Ian shrugged off his concern. "We'd never be hitting a ball in a pond."

"Who, us?" Dad said.

He and Ian chuckled.

"Maybe Biddy and I'll join you. At least at Saint Andrews. We can check out William and Kate's hangouts from their university days. Or I might take a few golf lessons. Been wanting to learn to play."

Dad quirked a skeptical brow. I'd never showed the slightest interest in golf, which tied with darts for the biggest snooze fest on TV.

"I could give you a lesson or two," Andrew said.

"On how *not* to hit a golf ball into a pond?" I teased.

"Sadly, I haven't figured that one out myself yet." The corners of his mouth curled into a playful grin.

I let out a soft giggle.

Could I be a bigger flirt?

Still smiling, Andrew excused himself to go outside and make a phone call.

Dad eyed me. "The only time I've seen you at all interested in golf was at the Murray reunion, when Ian gave you and Biddy each a green tweed purse with the Saint Andrews course logo embroidered on the front."

I peered over at Ian. "I adore that purse."

Ian laughed, a dimple creasing his cheek. "You're not getting off that easily. It's a different *Andrew* we're interested in hearing about."

"It certainly is," Dad said.

"I haven't a clue what you mean."

Dad and Ian started giggling, imitating me.

"You two are awful." I strolled off with a goofy grin, my dads still giggling.

I joined Gretta and Rosie, who were admiring the gingerbread castle.

Gretta slipped an arm around my shoulder. "And you didn't think you could even be decorating cookies. What a perfect day. A good thing I fought for that last jar of nutmeg, isn't it now?"

I nodded. "It was a good thing *you* fought hard to find your grandson."

"As did you," Gretta said.

"Thank you." Rosie became weepy. "For everything."

We shared a group hug.

Gretta handed me a small gift. I removed the tissue paper to find four pieces of whole nutmeg glued together, hanging from a green ribbon. One red number on each nutmeg, together spelling out the year 2022.

I laughed. "I love it."

Probably best not to tell her about Birdie's ornament on my tree, which I'd placed toward the back until next year.

Perhaps Gretta's animosity toward her cousin will have diminished a bit by then.

Andrew walked back into the room. Our gazes locked, and we shared a smile. My heart rate kicked up a notch, my breathing quickening.

"Nice to see the two of you getting on so well," Gretta said. "Since he'll likely be spending some time here."

"Indeed," Rosie said. "Maybe you should see if he has plans for New Year's Eve."

"I don't need a date for New Year's Eve."

I was staying home and wallowing in self-pity with a large pan of lasagna. Yet I couldn't help but smile. If Grandma were alive, she'd be flirting with the idea of Andrew and me. There was no relationship. Not yet...

Tommy joined his grandson, giving him a pat on the back. Both of them motorcycle enthusiasts, they were already making plans to attend the annual motorcycle race on the Isle of Man in June. The men chatted a moment, then Andrew approached us, wearing an uneasy look.

"I returned Maeve's calls," he said.

She'd left Andrew a half dozen messages this past week. Telling him about Maeve's panicked reaction to Stella and the GenDNA plot had softened him a bit toward his mother.

Gretta nibbled nervously on her lower lip. "How'd you get on?"

"We're meeting in a few weeks to talk. I need time to process it all. Seeing Mags's relationship with her dad and Ian, I'm not ready to throw mine away with Maeve. I'm not sure *what* I'm ready for at this point."

Gretta gave his hand a squeeze. "And you don't need to know. Give it time, luv."

Andrew repairing his relationship with Maeve would undoubtedly help Gretta and her daughter reconnect.

"It'll be grand." Rosie gave him a reassuring smile.

Biddy and Collin sauntered over, eating the gingerbread cookies Rosie had brought in case anyone was tempted to nibble on the castle.

"*Bonjour*," Biddy said. "*Ca va?*"

"Regret giving her the phrase book?" I asked Collin.

He smiled. "*Mais non.*"

I laughed.

"What are you doing for New Year's Eve?" Collin asked Andrew. "Mags doesn't have plans."

I shot Collin a mortified look. "Excuse me—I think I can find my own date." My gaze darted to Andrew. "Not that spending New Year's together would be a *date*."

"That'd be lovely, but I have plans," he said.

"Oh." Disappointment filled my voice.

Gretta's gaze narrowed on her grandson. "Important ones, are they?"

He nodded. "A mate's flying in from Australia. Haven't seen him in five years."

A *man*, not a *woman*, made me feel better.

Gretta's look grew more determined. "Well, couldn't you—"

"Let's go check on Tommy and Edmond." Rosie linked her arm with Gretta's, and the women strolled off.

"Thinking I might pop over to Dalwade Castle when you're there in January," Andrew said. "Check out that grave I adopted."

I struggled to keep the excited grin off my face.

Collin and Andrew discussed the March wedding at the castle and going to Glasgow afterward.

"You could be coming to Paris with us," Biddy told me.

"I'm not that pathetic, thank you. I'll be fine. Will finally start reading the books from Kiernan Moffat."

"Right, then. Romantic letters between Queen Victoria and her husband, Albert, are going to make ya feel better about being alone on New Year's Eve."

"That's not what the letters are about. They're a collection of her official communications, not her personal ones." At least I thought they were.

"I guess it's better than last New Year's. You becoming Jack Nicholson from *The Shining* at some remote Maine inn with spotty internet and cell service."

"It wasn't remote, and it was a lovely Victorian house."

"Still a good thing ya didn't sell your granny's house. Instead of turning into a crazed lunatic, you're like that fella in the Christmas movie. The one where the angel shows him what people's lives would have been like if he'd never existed."

*"It's a Wonderful Life?"*

"That's the one. Look at all the lives you've changed for the better. I'd never have gotten over Collin kissing that wretched Aisling Donnell when we were fifteen if it weren't for you convincing me that holding a grudge was silly. Thanks to you, we're together and going to Paris." She peered over at Collin with a dreamy look on her face.

They'd hooked up when Biddy and I had been investigating the missing Brendan Quigley manuscript Collin's family had inherited.

"Edmond and Rosie wouldn't be engaged." She gestured to the couple sharing a tender moment.

They'd rekindled their friendship when Rosie had assisted with solving the same mystery.

"And now Rosie has a grandson, a connection to her beloved Sean. She once again has a family." Biddy peered over at Dad and Ian, laughing. "Haven't seen your dad so happy in years. If you'd been working some temp job in the US, ya wouldn't have attended the Clan Murray reunion and discovered your biological father. And proven him innocent of his brother's murder. He might have been spending Christmas in prison. Forever."

That was an unsettling thought.

"Gretta never would have taken a DNA test and found her grandson. You've quite likely reunited her and Maeve. And you never would have met Andrew."

"We're not dating."

Biddy rolled her eyes. "You never looked at Finn, Josh, or any fella the way you do Andrew. And what's with that giggle? You haven't giggled like that since ya were ten. Not only is he handsome and witty, but patient. How many fellas would listen to ya go on for hours about dead people?"

I smiled at Andrew and Collin laughing.

"And there's that daffy grin." Biddy gave my arm a playful swat. "I'm right though, aren't I? You've brought everyone here together."

"No wonder I've been so tired lately. Guess it's a good thing I'm staying home New Year's Eve. Rather than reading, I'm going to catch up on my sleep."

"That's grand. Then ya can get crackin' the next day.

More lives to change in the new year." Biddy gave me a hug. "Can't imagine my life without you."

I couldn't imagine mine without Biddy...or every person in the room for that matter. Not only had I impacted their lives, they'd changed mine.

I stood by the ash tree in my backyard, peering at the house lit up inside, the chimney puffing white peat-scented clouds into the purplish-pink evening sky. Laughter carried out from the house, warming my face from the chilly breeze. I smiled at how well Dad, Ian, and Andrew were getting on. Pinky snorted an impatient grunt, standing in the long grass next to me.

I eyed the sheep. "Haven't learned how to open the fairy door yet? Smarty pants."

At the base of the tree trunk, I opened the tiny weathered red door with painted yellow bees, tucked a green slip of paper into the hiding space, and removed a blue one.

"May you get all your wishes but one so you always have something to strive for." Grandma had recited the Irish saying nineteen years ago when we'd put on the fairy door.

A year ago my wish to help Finn identify his biological father had reignited my passion for genealogy, having assisted Grandma with her research when I was young.

Following that one, four more wishes were granted.

To be financially able to maintain Grandma's house.

To feel like a Ballycaffey local.

To find my biological father.

To have an amicable relationship with Ian. However, I let

nature take its course and had felt Mom rather than the fairies was watching over me and that she'd work her magic.

After Grandma passed away, I'd removed the wadded ball of colored slips of paper from behind the fairy door. The ink had washed out, making them impossible to read. At the time, the only wish I could remember having written years ago was wanting to live with Grandma rather than my parents. Suddenly, I recalled a second wish. That I'd wanted to grow up to be just like Grandma.

My wish had come true.

# Genealogy Research Tips

The following genealogy research article is from my nonfiction book, *Genealogy Tips & Quips*. In 2018 I began writing a genealogy column for my monthly author newsletter about my personal research experiences. I was writing articles faster than I was publishing newsletters, so I decided to compile them into a book. *Genealogy Tips & Quips* includes fifty articles and two extensive case studies—one about how a paternal DNA test revealed my family's royal lineage, and my quest to uncover family secrets. I hope you find the tip helpful.

You can learn more about the book at www.elizawatson.com/genealogy-tips-and-quips.

# Tracing Your Family Backward

## AND THEN FORWARD TO FIND LIVING RELATIVES

I'm surprised at the number of family historians who spend years tracing their family trees back generations to their ancestors' homelands and then quit. When I reach that point, I celebrate with a glass of wine and begin tracing my ancestors' family members forward in hopes of one day sharing a pint with living relatives in Ireland. Over the past ten years, I've met numerous Irish relations from three of my family lines and have enjoyed many pints. I've learned family history—including a few family secrets—that I would never have uncovered on Ancestry.com. I have exchanged priceless family photos. And best of all, I've visited our ancestors' childhood homes, which I recount in Tip 49, "Walking in Your Ancestors' Footsteps: Finding Their Family Homesteads." I've used several methods to locate relatives, including connecting with an owner of an Ancestry.com family tree, traditional genealogy methods, and online super-sleuthing.

At the beginning of this book, I mentioned tracing my Daly line forward thanks to unrelated genealogist Jane Daly locating a 1960 newspaper article about Michael Daly's daughter (my Patrick's niece) having been struck and killed by a truck. With help from the internet, I found a descendant who belonged to a local Lions Club, and a board member put me in touch with my first living relative in Ireland.

Next, I traced another one of Michael's daughters forward. Using the Irish Newspaper Archives, www.irishnewsarchive.com, I pieced together birth, marriage, and death records for a daughter who married and had three children. I discovered that her one daughter married a reverend, and I was able to locate his church. Unfortunately, it turned out he'd passed away a year prior, in 2008, but my relation Joyce was still living in that same area. Thanks to an article on the church's website, I found the first picture of a living Irish relative. I sent Joyce a letter and received a lovely response. She put me in touch with her niece Charlotte, who had done a bit of research on the Dalys, including locating the family home in County Westmeath. Two years later on a trip to Ireland, I met Joyce and her two children, William and Patricia, along with Charlotte and Peter.

Back in 2008 I began piecing together my Flannery family tree. It was a bit challenging since the earliest surviving Roman Catholic records for my ancestors' parish in County Mayo dated from 1838. As luck would have it, the family members that emigrated were born prior to that year. This made it critical that I obtain every bit of information I could here in the US. That included marriage and birth records from Baltimore, where the family first lived before settling in Wisconsin. Luckily, the parents and five adult sons' families moved to the same area in southern Wisconsin. However, one son remained in Baltimore. A descendant of his and I have shared research and kept in touch.

Once I compiled as much information as I could, I began comparing my tree with others on Ancestry.com. After a bit of searching, I found someone in the US related to my Flannerys back six generations. I reached out to him and discovered that he'd recently visited our Flannerys' homeland, where he'd met a relative, Patrick Flannery. He was kind enough to put me in touch with Patrick, who would turn out to be the first Irish relative I'd meet.

Out of Patrick *Coffey's* eight known siblings, I successfully traced six of them forward. Three had immigrated to America, while three had remained in County Westmeath, Ireland. Luckily, his brother Andrew stayed in their hometown, where he had several children who lived to adulthood. Three of them remained in Ireland, but only one married and had children. Thankfully, this daughter, Catherine, was born and married in Andrew's home parish. In the 1901 and 1911 censuses, Catherine's family lived in County Offaly. After locating a 1930s marriage record for her daughter, I was off and running. Her married surname was an uncommon one, making the family easier to trace. Her obituary noted the names of two living sons. Bingo!

Using Ireland's online phonebook and people-search sites, I obtained the addresses of several potential candidates with the sons' names. I mailed letters to a half dozen possibilities and waited anxiously for a response. Thankfully, a letter made it into one of the son's mailboxes. Although he wasn't interested in genealogy, he kindly forwarded my letter to his brother, Bernard, who was interested. Bernard had limited information on his grandma Catherine, so I shared my research, and he shared some lovely photos, including one of his grandma's family circa 1900. I've enjoyed high tea at a fancy Dublin hotel with Bernard and his wife, Nuala. My husband and I recently celebrated Christmas with their entire family. But my most memorable moment with Bernard was when we located and then visited our Coffey ancestors' homesteads.

*Genealogy Tips & Quips*
Learn About Ancestry Research

Now Available

# Author's Note

Thank you so much for reading *How to Pursue a DNA Clue*. If you enjoyed Mags and Biddy's adventures, I would greatly appreciate your taking the time to leave a review. Reviews encourage potential readers to give my stories a try, and I would love to hear your thoughts. My monthly newsletter features genealogy research advice, my latest news, and frequent giveaways. You can subscribe at www. elizawatson.com. Thanks a mil!

# About Eliza Watson

When Eliza isn't traveling for her job as an event planner or tracing her ancestry roots through Ireland and Scotland, she is at home in Wisconsin working on her next novel. She enjoys bouncing ideas off her husband, Mark, and her cats, Frankie and Sammy.

Connect with Eliza Online
www.elizawatson.com
www.facebook.com/ElizaWatsonAuthor
www.instagram.com/elizawatsonauthor

CPSIA information can be obtained
at www.ICGtesting.com
Printed in the USA
BVHW020231281222
655124BV00021B/272